THE HAUNTING OF SARAH LESSINGHAM

MARGARET JAMES

THE HAUNTING OF SARAH LESSINGHAM

ST. MARTIN'S PRESS
NEW YORK

LEE COUNTY LIBRARY
SANFORD, N. C.

First published in the United States of America in 1978
Copyright © 1977 by Margaret James
All rights reserved. For information, write:
St. Martin's Press, Inc., 175 Fifth Ave., New York, N.Y. 10010.
Manufactured in the United States of America
Library of Congress Catalog Card Number: 77-9168

Library of Congress Cataloging in Publication Data

The haunting of Sara Lessingham.

   I. Title.
PZ4.B4734Hau   1978   [PR6052.E533]   823'.9'14   77-9168
ISBN 0-312-36424-5

ACKNOWLEDGMENTS

I am deeply grateful to the following authors from whose works I have been able to get a fascinating glimpse of Victorian life, and without whose scholarship I should not have been able to write this novel:

The Best Circles	Leonore Davidoff
Life in Victorian London	L. C. B. Seaman
The Early Victorian Woman	Janet Dunbar
Victoria's Heyday	J. B. Priestley
The Victorian Household	Marion Lochhead
Twice Round the Clock	George Augustus Sala
The Victorian Child	F. Gordon Roe
The Story of the Nursery	Magdalen King-Hall
Human Documents of the Victorian Golden Age	E. Royston Pike
Book of Household Management	Mrs. Isabella Beeton
The World of Victoriana	James Norbury
Victoriana	James Laver
Victorian England	W. J. Reader
Victorian People	Gillian Avery
London's Underworld	Henry Mayhew (Ed. by Peter Quennell)
Mayhew's London	Henry Mayhew (Ed. by Peter Quennell)
The Victorian Underworld	Kellow Chesney
Personal Reminiscences of a Great Crusade	Josephine Butler
Leisure & Pleasure in the 19th Century	Stella Margetson
The Workhouse	Norman Longmate
The Age of Consent: Victorian Prostitution and its Enemies	Michael Pearson
Skittles	Henry Blythe
The Courtesans—The Demi-Monde in Nineteenth Century France	Joanna Richardson
Useful Toil	Ed. by John Burnett

ONE

On a dark December afternoon in 1858, Sara Lessingham, aged seven, arrived in Candle Square. She pressed her nose against the carriage window, secure in the knowledge that as she was travelling alone, there was no one to rebuke her for her inquisitiveness, nor frown at her for twisting round in an unlady-like manner on the slippery leather seat. She felt very grown-up and important in her small, self-contained world which smelt of tobacco and rumbled along on complaining wheels through the Kensington streets.

In the whole of her life she had not travelled so great a distance before. There had been no reason to leave the sprawling old house in the Sussex countryside, and the weekly journey to church by dog-cart, or a special jaunt to a nearby town to see the shops, had been the limit of Sara's adventuring. But now she was in London, and it was Christmas Eve.

As the carriage turned into the Square she could see the tall, porticoed houses with their shining brass knockers and sturdy iron railings; the gas-lamps blurred and yellowish behind the veil of snow which had been falling steadily since noon. There were a few passers-by; brave spirits, bending their heads to the wind, clutching in their arms mysterious parcels wrapped in bright paper.

She was about to sink back on the seat when she saw the couple beneath the lamp-post. The woman was young and beautiful, wrapped in furs. Sara knew instinctively that if she had been close enough she would have smelt a light, fragrant perfume. The man was laughing down at her, brushing a snowflake away from her cheek, a protective hand over hers.

"Mama?"

Sara realised that she had said the word aloud, but there was no one to hear her, for the coachman was deafened by the clatter of the horses and carriage, too anxious to reach his destination to bother with the small girl in his charge.

Sara could feel the tears in her eyes, and suddenly all the expectant happiness was gone. How could she have been so stupid? How could she have imagined, even for a second, that it had been her mother? She shivered, hugging her blue pelisse about her, conscious for the first time that day of the intense cold.

Her mother was dead; her father too. She must learn to accept that. It was now three long months since that dreadful night; plenty of time to have grown used to the awfulness of the truth.

Even now, Sara was not really sure what had happened. That afternoon in early October had been like any other. She and her father had gone for a walk in the woods which lay beyond the garden. When they returned, tea had been ready by the fire in the sitting-room. She could remember everything about that last day, even the tiniest detail. How she and her father had shed their coats and muddy shoes, his deep laugh echoing her excited giggle, as they made their way to the low-ceilinged room with white walls and shabby furniture. Sara loved the room, with its comfortable old chairs, polished brasses and sketches drawn by her father.

Her mother had been dreaming by the fire, her gentle face flushed by its glow, toasting crumpets and waiting for the kettle on the hob to boil. They had teased her lovingly, and she had embraced them both with the warmth of her smile.

Sara's face grew pinched. She did not want to remember any more, for that was where the happiness ended, but the nightmare was crowding in on her again from all sides. The sight of the stranger's face had aroused thoughts which she had tried desperately to thrust out of her mind.

She shut her eyes, squeezing them hard, but she could still

see the glare of the flames and smell the acrid smoke in her nostrils. Someone had been screaming, crying out for help. There had been noise and confusion and shouting, and then a terrible kind of silence.

Sometime afterwards, they told Sara that she had been ill. A gaunt-looking woman in black bombazine, who said she was housekeeper to Sara's grandfather, had come to sit by her bed. Her grandfather was too old to care for her, she was told, and she would have to go to London to live with her mother's sister. The housekeeper had not been unkind. Indeed, she had tried to offer some sort of solace, but Sara had buried her head in her pillow and would not listen to what she was saying. When she got better, she had tried to get Mrs. Marsham, with whom she was staying, to tell her what had happened, but her questions were quickly turned aside.

She dreaded the nights most, for it was then that she had the bad dreams, fighting to wake herself to escape from the sight of things which she would never speak of to anyone. She thought Mrs. Marsham had looked at her pensively at times, but she could never summon up enough courage to ask her what she was thinking. And now it was too late. Now, she was in London.

Furtively Sara wiped her tears away. It would not do for her aunt and uncle to see her crying, for they would think her ungrateful. She had been told how lucky she was that they had offered her a good home, and that but for their generosity she would have found herself in the workhouse. She had no idea what a workhouse was, but the word had a hollow sound to it, and she straightened her shoulders as the carriage came to a halt and the driver got down from his perch to help her to alight.

Sara had a brief impression of a well-appointed hall with a plush carpet underfoot and a handsome mahogany hall-stand flanked by two carved chairs. Then the plump maid in a spotless cap and apron was opening another door, ushering Sara into the drawing-room where a small group of people sat quietly by the fireside.

Sara thought she had never before seen a room with so much furniture in it. Used to the simplicity of her father's home, she was overwhelmed by the lavishness of the dark red paper on the walls and the wealth of gilt-framed paintings. The floor was covered in a carpet of floral design, the tall windows draped with velvet curtains fringed with silk bobbles. Between two well-upholstered sofas, a piano, and numerous brocaded armchairs, there were half a dozen small tables crowded with ornaments of china, glass and silver. There were footstools, a heavy brass fender, an ornate coal-bucket and a vast mirrored overmantel bearing yet more knick-knacks.

She tore her bemused gaze away from the dazzling splendour to look again at those who waited to greet her. She had a quick impression of each of them. The woman lying on one of the sofas was so like Sara's mother that Sara caught her breath. She had the same rich brown hair, carefully dressed and drawn back to the nape of her neck, the same hazel eyes, good bones and long slender neck. But there the likeness ended, for Aunt Rachel's face was lined with boredom and discontent. The man by her side was thick-set and well-groomed in his dark frock-coat and narrow striped trousers, his light-coloured hair growing thin on top, his beard neatly trimmed. He had a reddish complexion and blue eyes and, despite the expensive clothes and luxury of his setting, he looked earthy and a trifle common.

The boy, of some eleven years, was clearly his son. His pale hair and eyes were a reflection of his father's, but he had a decidedly superior air about him, staring through Sara as if she did not exist.

The last member of the group sat slightly apart, working on an embroidery frame. She was plainly dressed in faded blue, with mid-brown hair scraped back from a high forehead, giving her face a bare and bony aspect. Her light grey eyes and sandy lashes added to her colourless appearance.

"Welcome, my dear."

Arthur Hardwin Grey rose from his chair and took Sara's hand in his, smiling down at her encouragingly as he led her towards the sofa.

"This is your Aunt Rachel, and this your cousin Oliver." He half-turned his head to the other woman, as if he had just remembered her existence. "Oh, and this is Miss Thorne, our housekeeper and companion to your aunt."

Mercy Thorne raised her head and looked at him, her needle stilled for a moment. She felt the resentment burn inside herself at Grey's introduction, even though it was only to a child. When she had first come to his house eight years ago, Arthur had been glad enough to acknowledge that she was his cousin, albeit a distant one, but then, of course, he had desperately wanted her services. Now he talked of her as one of the servants, although she had vigorously fought his attempts to relegate her to their ranks, winning a number of small concessions including her right to eat with the family, except when they were entertaining, and to possess her own poky little room near the top of the house.

She scarcely spared a second glance for Sara. She was just another child, easily dealt with. Instead her gaze turned on Rachel and her bloodless lips moved in faint scorn. After four children and two miscarriages, Rachel Grey had fallen back on poor health to escape the wearisome burden of domesticity and, Mercy suspected, the attentions of her husband. It was simpler to lie on her couch, relating imaginary ailments to her friends, than to run the house or attempt to compete with Arthur's business affairs which kept him in the city for most of his time. Although Arthur was in trade, it was one of the more respectable kinds, accepted by the peers of his own strata of society, and most decidedly profitable. Mercy thought Rachel a fool. No wonder Arthur spent so little time with his wife. What man would, faced with constant whining and complaints? She let her bleached lashes fall again, bending her head over her work as Grey said jovially:

"So you're Austin Lessingham's daughter. Not much like

your father, are you? Perhaps you favour your mother; pretty woman I always thought."

"Arthur!"

Rachel frowned. She had not particularly wanted her sister's child, but she could not be bothered to argue about it, and Arthur had seemed strangely insistent that they should take her in. After all, Sara would not worry her. Mercy and the servants would care for her but, since she was there, Rachel saw no reason to torment the girl with reminders of her recent loss. It proved yet again how lacking Arthur was in sensitivity.

"Eh?" Grey looked blank for a moment; then he shrugged. "Sorry, m'dear. I forgot. Can't quite get used to the notion that . . . well . . . these things happen."

He gave a quick cough and changed the subject.

"Well now, Sara, I hope you'll be happy with us. Do you think you will be?"

Sara swallowed her misery, more hurt by her aunt who was so like her mother and yet so different, than by her uncle's unthinking bluntness.

"Yes, uncle." She whispered the words, trying not to let them see the quiver of her lips. "I was told that I must be grateful to you and Aunt Rachel."

"Were you indeed?" Grey gave a sudden friendly grin. "Who told you that?"

"Mrs. Marsham."

"Who is she?"

"She looked after me when . . . when. . . ."

"Ah yes." Grey moved on hurriedly, conscious at last of his niece's overbright eyes. "Yes, well, no doubt you will be. We'll do all we can for you, you know. Your father left some money; just enough for your upbringing. Pity your grandfather lost his fortune. You'd have been a rich gel."

"Arthur!"

"Well, it's true."

Grey gave his wife a slightly exasperated look. Rachel did not like to be reminded that her father had made a fool of himself and lost everything in unwise speculations. She prided herself on the status of her family, which she regarded as infinitely superior to her husband's. Grey pulled a face. Her sister had been as rash as their father. With beauty and brains, she had still married Austin Lessingham, a struggling artist with no prospects, when she could have used her natural gifts to snare a wealthy industrialist or even a peer, had she chosen to do so. It had been a terrible waste. He looked back at Sara.

"All that your grandfather left you was a small remembrance. Some trinket or trifle which was saved when the crash came, no doubt. You'll get it when you are eighteen. Well, never mind, I've enough to fill up the gaps."

He coughed again, catching the look in his wife's eye, and took a heavy gold watch from his waistcoat pocket.

"Nearly five o'clock. No time for you and Oliver to be here talking of such things. It's Christmas Eve, and there's plenty to do in the playroom. Oliver, take your cousin up to meet the others. Come, Sara, kiss your aunt good-night."

Hesitantly Sara approached the sofa. It was uncanny to be so near to such a familiar face and to find it devoid of love. She felt Rachel Grey's withdrawal and wished she could run away, but then Rachel proffered a reluctant cheek and Sara managed to plant a feather-light kiss on it, turning in confusion to follow Oliver to the door.

When they had gone, Grey ran a reflective finger over his moustache.

"Pretty child. She'll be a beauty one day, mark my words."

Rachel gave him a hard look. She did not like Arthur to refer to other women's beauty, even that of a child of seven.

"She is too thin."

"She won't stay thin. Wait till she fills out a bit."

"Really, Arthur, sometimes you are so coarse."

"Nothing coarse about beauty."

He smiled down at her sardonically. Pity Rachel had grown so stout. It was lying about all day that had done it, of course. That, and her hearty appetite. She'd been lovely enough when he had married her. It had not only been that he wanted to better himself by a good marriage; he'd wanted Rachel too. Even now her dark hazel eyes and flawless skin were ravishing, and he would have tolerated a bit of excess flesh if only she would put aside the absurd notion that she was always ill. It irritated and bored him, and he only made love to her now and then as a matter of duty, conscious that she hated every moment of it and thought him gross in his demands.

"You're not going out, Arthur?"

Rachel's voice was querulous, tinged with a possessiveness which grated on his ear. She might not welcome his attentions, but she was never willing to let him go for all that.

"No, my dear, not to-night. To-night is Christmas Eve. Wear something nice at dinner; it's a special occasion."

He went out humming lightly to himself, and Rachel said tautly:

"How thoughtless he is. How can I think of clothes at such a time? Doesn't he realize that I am not well?"

"I am sure he does." Mercy did not raise her head. She had heard the question so often that she had a number of stock answers ready to combat it. "He is busy."

"He should find time for me. I am his wife."

"I'm sure he doesn't forget it."

Rachel's lips compressed to a thin line. She could hear the implied criticism in Mercy's voice, but it was no use quarrelling with her. She had tried that in the past, for she had never liked the woman and resented her presence in her home, but Mercy could make life uncomfortable in small, irritating ways. A torn gown not mended in time for an important party; a favourite brooch mislaid; a meal not quite up to standard. Rachel lay back against the cushions and stifled her anger.

"Will that child get on with the others, do you think?"

"I'm certain she will. She seems a quiet little thing. There is a look of you about her."

"She is more like my sister when she was young."

"Is that why... ?"

Mercy broke off abruptly, but Rachel gave a short laugh. Sometimes, when they were alone, she was completely honest with Mercy for it was too much trouble to dissemble.

"Why I did not want her to come here, do you mean? Perhaps. Beth was always my father's favourite. He gave her everything she wanted. When I married, father cared even less about me. He didn't like Arthur, and said he wasn't good enough for me, and he was right of course. Yes, Beth was the one he really loved."

"But in the end it did her no good, did it?"

Rachel's face paled slightly and the look of chagrin was gone.

"No. No, I suppose not. I shall be good to her; Sara, I mean."

"I know you will." Mercy's eyes met Rachel's for a brief moment, a faint smile curling the corners of her mouth. "You are good to us all, Rachel dear. Now, may I get you a glass of sherry before dinner?"

Sara followed Oliver upstairs, staring about her with awe. The first floor of the house continued to amaze with its rich Turkey carpets, bright gasoliers and polished tables on the landing.

On the second floor the grandeur vanished, and drugget and grubby distemper replaced the extravagance below. Here, the gas-lights were dimmer and the landing and corridors seemed to stretch on for ever, as if there were no walls to curtail their wanderings.

"It is very big, isn't it?"

She ventured the question at last as they came to a stop outside one of the rooms. She was rather afraid of Oliver, but at least he was looking at her now and seeing her as a person.

"Of course."

Oliver was studiedly off-hand. He hadn't really wanted another female to clutter his small world, but at least this one was quiet and satisfyingly impressed by her new surroundings. He thought she would not be too much trouble to tame. She would soon learn, as his sisters had learned, that he was the master of the playroom, and that his orders had to be obeyed if dire consequences were not to follow.

"There's another floor above this. See, there are the stairs."

Sara looked nervously at the shadowed arch, where twisting steps led away into nothingness. She moistened her lips which had grown suddenly dry. She could feel the cold all about her, wishing she were home again where everything was safe and familiar, but, of course, there was no home now. Just a pile of charred timber, or so Mrs. Marsham had whispered to one of her friends when she thought Sara had not been listening. She put the memory firmly out of her mind, pretending an interest she did not feel.

"What is up there?"

"Nothing much." Oliver raised his shoulders. "Just a room or two. No one goes up there, but sometimes we hear the stairs creak at night."

He said it casually, and Sara looked at him quickly, wondering why he was not afraid.

"Why do they creak, if no one goes up there?"

He saw her fear and played on it, a small secret smile on his lips.

"Who knows? Better not to ask if you're afraid of spirits."

"Spirits!"

Her mouth opened in consternation, but now Oliver had tired of the subject and was pushing her inside the playroom, anxious to return to his task of supervising the preparations for Christmas.

After the opulence of the drawing-room, the playroom was positively shabby, but Sara's heart slowed to a normal beat as she saw the roaring fire behind the high guard, the long red curtains at the window muffling the sound of the wind, and the faded, but still serviceable, carpet of blue, patterned with nosegays of pink roses. There were desks and a table at one end, for this was also the schoolroom, a range of cupboards and shelves along one wall, and a rocking-chair beside the hearth. The walls were a dull, washed-out blue, but that didn't matter now for they were hung with branches of holly and mistletoe. In the centre of the room there was a small Christmas tree, shining with transluscent baubles and alight with shimmering tinsel. On top of a wooden chest was a pile of parcels of all shapes and sizes, tied up with coloured ribbons and twine.

Here, there were more people to meet. Amy Harris, the governess, a good-natured girl with coppery hair and an overblown figure, and Mary Hopper, the second maid, just seventeen and glad to have found a good position for herself with a well-to-do respectable family. They were kneeling on the floor, wrapping up more gifts, smiling at Sara and welcoming her as they bade her take off her pelisse and help them with their work.

Oliver introduced her to his brother and sisters with a proprietary air, as if she were a new piece of property which he had just acquired, and was anxious to exhibit. Sidney, a year younger than Oliver, very much like his mother. Henrietta, fourteen; quiet and withdrawn in a print frock billowed out over layers of petticoats. She did not look like her mother or her father, and was rather plain with a sallow skin and dark eyes. Rebecca, the youngest, aged eight; plump and rosy and pretty, with a slightly sulky mouth.

They greeted Sara politely enough, accepting her into their circle without comment, leaving it to Oliver, the leader, to put her to work on wrapping up a shawl for cook in a piece of glossy green paper.

When all the packages were ready there was hot chocolate to drink, served in plain white mugs, with slices of delicious walnut cake and tiny biscuits with frosted tops.

They sat on the floor round the fire, toasting their feet, listening to the snow beat against the window. Sara was feeling sleepy, for it had been a long day.

"Sara has a legacy."

Oliver took a bite out of his cake and made the announcement in a tone which commanded instant attention. They all looked at him, rousing themselves to listen.

"What is a legacy?"

Sidney was yawning, rubbing his eyes, but aware that Oliver would expect some reaction.

"A kind of present."

"What sort of present?"

"No one knows. A trinket or a trifle, father says."

"How do you know?" Henrietta was sceptical. She knew she should have been the one to take the lead, because she was the eldest, but Oliver had usurped her position with ease. She accepted the situation because she was proud of her brother, but now and then she made it her business to challenge him.

"Are you making it up?"

"Of course not. I told you; father said so. Grandfather left it to her."

"Did he leave me one too?" Rebecca said it quickly, piqued by the thought that she might have been missed out. "What did he leave me?"

"Nothing." Oliver was blunt, ignoring her greed. "Only to Sara."

"Why?" Rebecca's mouth grew more sullen, her cake forgotten for the time being. She adored walnut cake, but the thought that Sara was to have something which she had been denied was too bitter to pass over. "Why didn't he leave me something too?"

"Now, Rebecca." Amy Harris was rocking herself gently back and forth, glad that the day was nearly over. She had been up at six, and the children had been over-excited and harder to handle than usual. "Oliver cannot answer that. Eat your cake, dear."

"I don't want to." Rebecca scowled. "And Oliver can answer anything."

Oliver looked pleased, smiling at his sister with approval.

"I expect because he didn't like father."

"Oliver!"

Mary Hopper smothered a giggle. Master Oliver was a caution, right enough. She had seen from the very first day she had started to work for Mrs. Grey that it would be foolish to fall out with him, and she always had a smile for Oliver, giving him just a little more of everything when serving luncheon, making sure that he understood she was his friend.

"It's true." Oliver gave Miss Harris a scornful look. "Everyone says so. Even mama says so; I've heard her." He returned to the others, for they were a more responsive audience than Amy Harris. "What do you think it will be? I say it will be a necklace."

"No, no, it will be a ring."

"I think it will be a brooch."

Amy Harris relaxed and took another sip of chocolate. The crisis was over. They had forgotten why Sara was the only child to be favoured in their grandfather's Will, too busy guessing what she would receive to pursue the uncomfortable truth about old Mr. Lorrimer's feelings for his son-in-law.

By eight o'clock the children were all ready for bed. To-morrow was Christmas, and they must get to sleep quickly or it would never come. Amy hustled the boys off to their room, even Oliver prepared to give way to her authority in view of the importance of the morrow.

The girls' room was very near to the arch which led to the upper floor. Mary Hopper wrapped a thick woollen shawl round Sara's shoulders and hurried her along the corridor. The room struck chill and unwelcoming after the warmth and cosiness of the playroom, and Sara's prayers were brief as she knelt beside the hard narrow bed and tried to ignore the lump in her throat.

"There you are, Miss Sara." Mary was tucking the bedclothes in with cheerful vigour. "Miss Henrietta and Miss Rebecca will be along in a minute, and then you'll be all right. Stay in bed, mind. Never know what you might see in this house at night."

Sara stared at her. The flame of the candle by the bed made Mary's face seem different. She looked older, the half-light painting lines round her eyes and mouth. Oliver had said odd things about that staircase, and now Mary was hinting at something.

"What . . . what do you mean, Mary? What kind of things?"

Mary pulled the cotton coverlet into place and straightened up, totally unaware of the terror in Sara's wide, round eyes.

"Well, they say the house is haunted. Never seen anythin' myself, of course, but I've heard noises. Maybe it's ghosts, maybe somethin' else. Who knows? Never you mind, Miss Sara. You go to sleep; to-morrow's Christmas Day."

Sara huddled beneath the bedclothes, willing Henrietta and Rebecca to hurry up, praying that they would arrive before the stairs started to creak.

The next night Sara lay in bed again. It was very late and she was exhausted by the excitement of the day. As she tried to rub her toes together to get them warm, she thought about all that had happened since eight o'clock that morning, when she had been woken by the shouts and cries of her cousins. After breakfast there had been church, with snow to crunch over on the way, and carols to sing in tune with the mellow organ up in the west gallery. Then the magic of gathering together in the dining-room, where the big Christmas tree stood on a table of its own, surrounded by parcels crying out to be opened. Uncle Arthur had been full of good humour, and even Aunt Rachel had forsaken her couch to enter into the spirit of things, helping to hand the gifts round, making suitable noises of pleasure as she unwrapped the embroidered handkerchiefs from Henrietta, the sampler from Rebecca and the real ivory fan from the boys.

Sarah had never seen such toys before, for money had been scarce at home. Miraculously, she found herself the proud possessor of a skipping rope with scarlet handles, a painted musical box which played a tinkling waltz, a Noah's Ark with a stream of small, carved animals, and a china doll whose eyes opened and shut, and who had a dress of blue silk with a fringed sash.

She had hardly been able to tear her attention away from her treasures to admire the others' presents, although she had seen the wisdom of exclaiming over Oliver's new peep-show, the set of ivory chessmen, and the mechanical man with a drum made of brass.

After that came luncheon, with roast turkey, stuffed with chestnuts and served with bread sauce; and a great plum pudding topped with brandy and set alight when the gasoliers were turned down. At five o'clock there was tea, although no one was really hungry. Finally, at nearly nine o'clock, there was supper in the playroom, with jellies, ice-cream, sweet biscuits covered with hundreds and thousands, and tall jugs of sweet lemonade.

Sara stirred in her bed, listening to the deep, regular breathing of Henrietta and Rebecca on the far side of the room. She was drifting towards sleep herself when she heard it; the unmistakable sound of the stairs. She sat bolt upright, straining her eyes in the darkness. No one could be there; it was far too late. She had heard her aunt and uncle on the floor below at least two hours ago, conscious of the whispers and footsteps of cook and the maids a little before that.

She did not realise that she had got out of bed until she found herself by the door. It was a strange compulsion which forced her to turn the knob and let the door swing in an inch or two, for her natural instinct was to hide from whatever it was outside.

There was nothing to be seen at first and she was just about to close the door again when she saw the flicker of a candle. Transfixed, she watched the light, seeing the misty white figure come into view for a brief second and then turn and pass through the archway. She did not wait for any more. She shut the door in a panic and rushed for the bed, narrowly avoiding a chair in her headlong flight. Under the covers, pulled high over her head, she crouched in a small ball, too frightened to move, certain she would never be able to close her eyes.

But at last drowsiness came, and with it the bad dreams again. Not of stairs which made noises, or figures in white which melted into the gloom, but of fire, raging and noisy and destructive as it burned away all the things she had loved so dearly. She cried out in her sleep, waking up abruptly to find her face wet with tears as she lay back hopelessly to wait for the morning.

At eight o'clock on Christmas Eve, Jane Briggs was in Henry Clarke's pawnshop in the Clerkenwell Road. She was fourteen years old, with auburn hair, a milk-white skin obscured by grime, and large green eyes which tilted gently at the outer corners.

The shop was crowded, for everyone wanted extra money at Christmas time, and she knew she would have to wait for half an hour or more before Mr. Clarke or his assistant, Jake, had time to consider her offering of a flat iron, a worn shawl and a pair of shabby boots.

But at least it was not cold inside. Jane was very familiar with the cramped little shop with its long, scarred counter and flimsy wooden partitions which were supposed to give privacy to those engaged in the vital business of raising a few coppers on their paltry possessions. Behind the counter were stacked the miscellany of goods which Mr. Clarke had accumulated over the last week, and which he had not yet had time to store in the damp cellar below. There were faded pictures and artificial flowers under glass domes; saucepans and kettles and pots of every kind; clothing of all shapes and sizes; knives, forks, fishing-rods, clocks, work-boxes, and even a pair of opera glasses.

When she had finally extracted sixpence from Jake, Jane left the smelly warmth of the pawnbroker's and made her way to Meggs Yard where she lived. Meggs Yard was in the heart of the rookery behind the Clerkenwell Road, comprising a dozen mean dwellings housing an uncounted number of human beings and an army of rats, mice, cockroaches and fleas. It boasted one decrepit shop, selling a few cheap goods essential to the maintenance of life.

Here Jane purchased two ounces of tea in a twist of paper, a scrap of rough sugar and a small quantity of milk. Then she had to face the snow again.

Jane lived in a house shared by four other families, where she, her mother, father, and six brothers and sisters crammed themselves into two narrow rooms. In the kitchen there was a stone floor, always oozing with damp, a sink in one corner and an apology for a fireplace which seldom saw more than a few lumps of coal and a handful of burning sticks. It had a dresser with some chipped pieces of crockery hanging on rusted nails, a table with one leg shorter than the others, and four battered chairs. In the adjoining room, where everyone slept, there were three mattresses; one for her father and mother, one for herself and her sisters, and a third for her brothers.

When Jane had time to dream, which wasn't very often, she pretended that she lived alone, for to her the greatest luxury of life seemed to be the joy of being by oneself. There was never a waking moment when she was not crowded by other human beings, as poor and as cold and as dirty as herself. By day, from seven-thirty in the morning until seven at night, she worked shoulder to shoulder with thirty girls of her own age in a local match factory. At night, she was never more than an inch away from her family. With the exception of her father, she was fond of them all, but she longed for privacy and the right to a reasonable amount of living space where no one else intruded.

She found her mother sweeping the floor. She looked tired, for after her day's work at the nearby clothing factory, she had sat up until two in the morning for the last three weeks, stitching at shirts to produce a few more coppers to provide scraps of meat, some vegetables and a fresh loaf of bread for Christmas. The stew smelled good on the hob which for once was heated by a decent coal fire.

Jane smiled at her mother and began to make the tea, miserly with the precious brown leaves, letting the cracked old pot draw nicely by the fire before pouring it out and lacing it with a dash of milk. She warmed herself for a moment, drying her skirt as she watched her sisters try to clean the dresser with a rag which put on more dirt than it removed. She was almost happy for a while, sipping her hot drink and feeling her cheeks burn. Then she heard the scuffle at the door and her heart sank.

Her father was drunk, of course, as he always was at that time of night, lurching into the kitchen and shouting at her mother as soon as he set eyes on her. This time his complaint was that his meal was not ready, spewing vile words at her as she shrank from him, finally hitting her across the face with his fist.

"Stop it!"

Jane rushed forward, unable to hold back in spite of the inevitable retribution. She had tried to prevent her father's violence before, and had paid the price for it, but somehow the sight of her mother cringing away, holding a bruised cheek, was too much for her. Her father swung round angrily, swaying on his heels.

"What's that? What d'yer say?" He tried to focus, waiting until her face became more than a white blur and he could see the condemnation in her bright green eyes. "D'yer dare to tell me to stop it? You bloody slut! What business is it of yours?"

"She's done nothing." Jane was on the defensive now, her hot wrath dying rapidly as she saw the look on his face. "You've no cause to hit her. There's food for you."

"You insolent bitch!"

He was unfastening the heavy leather belt from about his

waist, spitting in the corner as he abandoned his wife to deal with Jane. She backed away, keeping her eyes fixed on him, her mouth dry as he wound the strap round his hand. She had had many beatings from him in the past; those she had grown used to. But lately there had been something about the way he had looked at her when he pulled up her skirts to punish her that made her writhe in a different way. She did not understand her new fright, but she respected it, and when she saw him smile and reach out for her, she gave a quick cry and rushed past him to the door. She heard him raise his voice in a bellow, waiting only to listen to the crash as he tripped over a chair and measured his length on the floor. Then she slipped out of the house, running as hard as she could, looking back now and then to make sure that he was not following.

She did not know how long she ran. She was only conscious of the biting cold and her ravenous hunger. For a while she regretted her flight. After all, what was one more thrashing? When it was over, and her father had fallen into a drunken sleep, her mother would have given her some stew and a piece of bread. Now she had nothing.

Suddenly she became aware that she had left the slums of Clerkenwell behind. She did not know where she was, but it was clearly a better-class neighbourhood, with a few shops still open, and lights in a nearby café and public house. She was staring in the window of one of the shops, her stomach aching at the sight of the cakes and pastries laid out in tantalising rows, when a voice said quietly :

"Are you hungry, my dear?"

Jane turned quickly, her alarm dying down when she saw the middle-aged, motherly-looking woman eyeing her with concern.

"Yes."

She said it baldly, for there was no use in pretending, and the woman nodded compassionately.

"You look cold too. Haven't you got a coat?"

Jane shook her head and the woman clicked her tongue sympathetically.

"I tell you what." She was smiling brightly, patting Jane on the shoulder. "I'm just off home to have my supper. I've got a nice bit of fish and some roast mutton to follow. There's plenty for both of us, and maybe I can find something in my cupboard for you to wear. What do you say to that?"

For a moment Jane could say nothing. The thought of food and shelter and something dry to put on choked the words in her throat, and all she could do was to nod. The woman seemed satisfied with that, and took her arm.

"I'm Daisy Letchworth. Mrs. Daisy Letchworth. I live quite close by. How old are you, love?"

"Fourteen."

"Ah yes, a nice age. Couldn't be better. Are your parents alive?"

"No." Jane made the decision quickly. She did not know why she was so certain that her mother and father would be an encumbrance in the eyes of her new-found friend, but she could feel it in the air between them. "No, they're dead."

"No other relations?"

"None."

"Poor child."

Mrs. Letchworth said it absently, but she looked pleased, and before Jane could give the matter any more thought they were turning into the gate of a neat little house with Nottingham lace curtains at the window and a holly wreath pinned to the knocker.

The next hour passed in a dream. Jane was ushered into a cosily furnished parlour and allowed to warm herself at the blazing fire, while Mrs. Letchworth whispered instructions to the maid, who stared indifferently at Jane as if it were the most normal thing in the world for her mistress to come home with a starving waif in tow.

Then she had been taken upstairs and the maid had helped her to bath and wash her hair. Jane had never had a bath before, and she was frightened at first in case the water should lap over her and drown her. But the fear was unfounded, and the fat cake of soap smelt of violets, and soon she was revelling in the feel of the lather against her skin, the heat seeping through to her very bones.

When she was dry and her long hair brushed to smooth order, she found undergarments, stockings and a lavender-coloured frock laid out on the bed. She had never seen anything so beautiful before in all her life, and she almost cried as the maid helped her to get into the cotton and flannel petticoats which made the dress spread out as if she wore the fashionable crinoline.

It was whilst they were finishing a sweet trifle that Jane's bubble of happiness burst. At first, she was not sure what it was that Daisy Letchworth was saying, but then she understood, for she had not lived in a rookery in Clerkenwell for fourteen years for nothing. She stared at her benefactress, dumb with shock, letting the spoon fall from her fingers with a clatter.

"Come, dear, it's a simple question."

Daisy Letchworth sipped her port and lemon and looked at the girl with mild exasperation. She hoped she was not going to prove stupid or troublesome, after all the efforts she had made. She had seen the possibilities in Jane immediately, despite the girl's rags and dirty hair and face. The wetness had made the frock cling to the slight figure, emphasising the slim waist and small, upthrust breasts. Now that she was clean and properly clad, the child was positively stunning, and her eyes would be the undoing of many a man, or she, Daisy Letchworth, would eat her own Sunday bonnet.

"Well, are you a virgin?"

Jane took a deep breath and managed a quick nod. The decision had to be made instantly. There was no time to think things out and decide what was best to do. She either had to strip herself of her new clothes and don the limp rag again, venturing out into the pitiless snow once more, or she had to accept that Mrs. Letchworth was now about to claim her pound of flesh. For a short while she had thought it was merely kindness on Mrs. Letchworth's part, taking her in off the streets and feeding her, but she should have known better. There wasn't that amount of kindness in the whole world.

And when all was said and done, there wasn't much of a choice to make. In the end, she'd probably find herself the prey of the youths who hung about Meggs Yard, shouting obscenities at any woman below the age of forty. This way, she would at least embrace prostitution in comfort.

She nodded again, more definitely this time.

"Yes, I am."

"I have to be sure, you see. They're very fussy about that, you know."

"Who?"

"Why, my clients, of course." Mrs. Letchworth looked at her as if she thought her half-witted. "Can't be too careful about . . . well you know. They're all men of substance, with families. Can't have anything going wrong, can we?"

Jane had no idea what Daisy Letchworth was talking about, but she inclined her head, as if agreeing whole-heartedly with her sentiments, and after a moment Mrs. Letchworth said:

"Well, love, if you're ready I'll take you upstairs. He's due at twelve o'clock." She gave a discreet titter. "You'd think they'd want to be in their own homes, seeing that it's Christmas, wouldn't you? Never mind, better for us that they want to stray. Come along; this way."

Fifteen minutes later, Jane was sitting alone again in the bedroom. It was furnished modestly but with care, and she found time to admire the floral curtains and the dark green carpet before letting her gaze stray to the big bed with a patchwork quilt nearly touching the floor on each side of it.

He, whoever he was, would be there in ten minutes, so Mrs. Letchworth said. Jane pushed the unknown visitor out of her mind for a moment and considered other things which were assuming new and important proportions in her mind.

She had never before been conscious of her own body. It was something which had never needed to be thought about until now. In the bath that night she had seen it as though for the first time, and it had amazed and fascinated her. She glanced down at the loose wrap she wore, feeling the silk smooth against her skin. It was a new and rather splendid sensation, and she let one hand run down her thigh as if to make sure it was really her own.

Promptly at twelve o'clock the door opened and Jane got up slowly. The man who came into the room was short and stout, but very expensively dressed, with sleek black hair parted down the centre. He stared at Jane with frank interest as he began to remove his damp overcoat, flinging it over a chair. She returned the stare, aware that he smelled of expensive cigar smoke, and of some strong, pungent scent.

She was rather frightened, but she knew the final moment of decision had come. If she were to run past him now, she would spend the rest of her life in a living purgatory, like her mother. If she stayed, and could please him, there was no telling what advantages there might be, nor how far she could travel along the road of success.

Despite her youth and her total lack of experience, she knew it was a matter of confidence. Was she to be the mistress of this encounter, or he the master? She smiled at him, letting the wrap fall open an inch or two, suddenly supremely self-assured as she saw his face. He wanted her. She knew that at once, and her eyes crinkled up in amusement.

"Aren't you going to undress?"

She brushed her auburn hair over her shoulder, letting him see its length and silky quality. His eyes had widened a fraction and a faint line of perspiration was standing out on his forehead.

"If you don't undress, how will you feel my body through so many clothes?"

The man gave a quick laugh.

"You're a cool one, and no mistake." The smile faded, and

his voice was suspicious. "Are you sure you're a virgin, as Daisy says? I've not paid all that money for used goods, and I've heard times enough how these things can be faked."

She mocked his concern with the lightness of her voice.

"Of course I'm a virgin. Who should know better than me?"

She knew she could be impudent now, for she could feel his need of her and, besides, he wasn't a gentleman. There was no need to be afraid of him for all his fancy pomades and well-cut clothes.

She lay on the bed, opening the wrap and watching his face. It looked hungry, almost desperate, as he began to fumble with his waistcoat. She was not quite sure what to do, despite Mrs. Letchworth's hurried instructions, for she had never encountered a situation like this before. She had heard her father grunting and panting with her mother on their mattress, of course, and her mother's occasional moan, but this was different. She knew it would be quite different. But, after all, the man would know what to do, and she had always been quick to learn.

She waited until he stood naked by the side of the bed, then slowly she raised her arms and held them out to him.

TWO

At six o'clock on a morning in mid-October 1868, Jenny Brice, the housemaid at No. 11, Candle Square, made her way to the breakfast-room and opened the shutters.

This done, she moved the heavy steel fender and irons and sprinkled tea-leaves carefully over the carpet, brushing the dust towards the fireplace. When the last speck of dirt was gone, she spread a clean piece of sacking on the hearth, opening her housemaid's box, neatly packed with brushes, emery-paper, black lead and a leather. She worked swiftly, for there was a great deal to be done before breakfast. Mrs. Tamworth, the cook, was not expected to help upstairs, and so there was only she and Aggie Lowther, the parlour maid, to get the whole house ship-shape before the family began to come downstairs.

Although she dreaded getting up early on winter mornings, Jenny preferred to work alone, and liked to get as much done as possible before Miss Thorne appeared on the scene to run her finger along ledges in search of dust.

Jenny looked up as the door opened, and then gave a wide smile.

" 'Morning, Miss Sara. You're up early again."

"Good-morning, Jenny. Yes, I couldn't sleep."

Sara Lessingham at seventeen, rising eighteen, was the most beautiful girl Jenny had ever seen. She could never resist staring at the small proud head with the rich brown hair piled up in great coils at the back, and the perfect oval of the face with huge hazel eyes under gently arched brows. There was a faint pink flush along the cheekbones; the mouth full and lovely in its lines. Sara had an air of serenity about her, even when there were shadows beneath her eyes which betokened another disturbed night.

"Did you dream again?"

Jenny was sympathetic, brushing away as she spoke. An odd kind of understanding had grown up between the two young women, despite the difference in their stations. Since Sara often rose early, they met and talked when no one else was about, respecting each other and sharing an unspoken affection.

"Yes, I did." Sara was rueful, shivering slightly. "Yes, it is stupid of me, isn't it? Each night I swear I will not dream again, and every night I do."

"Every night?"

"Well, perhaps not every night." She gave a soft laugh. "Yes, you're right, Jenny, I exaggerate. I must stop feeling sorry for myself, for it's morning now."

"Just let me get this fire going, miss, and then I'll make you a cup of tea."

"Thank you."

Sara walked to the window and looked out. There was no one about yet, for it was too early, but she liked the Square when it was empty and one could see across the neat green patch in its centre to the houses on the far side. Candle Square had grown rather more fashionable during the ten years that Sara had lived there. It had never pretended to ape the ways of the great squares of Mayfair and Belgravia, satisfied with its own place in society, and smug in the knowledge that its inhabitants were prosperous, God-fearing, and undeniably respectable.

Sara closed her eyes, hearing the comforting noises which Jenny was making with the emery paper. Soon there would be other sounds as the house began to wake up. Mrs. Tamworth would come creaking down at about seven, grumbling about her rheumatism. Mercy would appear about the same time, with grey hair now and a sharper tongue, growing rather deaf. Aggie, plump but attractive for all that, was up already, of course, cleaning the servants' rooms, ready to descend on the master bedroom with cans of hot water at precisely eight o'clock, and then to attend to Aunt Rachel's breakfast tray.

After that the others would arrive. Henrietta would be first, for she was always punctual; still withdrawn as she had been as a child, and no prettier with the passing of time. Sara had never quarrelled with her elder cousin, but she could feel no warmth for her, for Henrietta seemed to shut everyone out of her life with an invisible wall. Oliver would be next. He was surprisingly handsome now, and the apple of his father's eye. He had started work in Grey's city office in the previous year, making excellent progress, or so Uncle Arthur insisted. Sidney was still at college, but home now for a few weeks after a bad chest complaint. He was thin and pale and coughed a lot, but he had proved himself an amiable companion, and Sara was fond of him. Rebecca, the spoilt one, would be last, of course. She had not quite lived up to the promise of her childhood beauty. She was comely enough, but something was lacking, and she tended to put on weight with frightening ease. She had always been jealous of Sara, and her envy had deepened when she had discovered that her father's friends tended to look first at Sara and then, as an afterthought, at her.

Finally Uncle Arthur would arrive in the breakfast-room at eight-thirty and unfold his copy of *The Times*, as Aggie and Jenny carried in the hot rolls and coffee, lifting the lids from the silver dishes which contained crisply-cooked bacon, eggs, sausages and kidneys. Sara thought he had changed least of all, for he did not look much older than when she had first seen him. Certainly he had grown a trifle stouter and was now nearly bald, but he had kept his brisk, cheerful manner and quick easy gait which she remembered from her first day. He had always been kind to her, treating her no differently from his own children. Indeed, at times he seemed to go out of his way to make a special fuss of her, as if to make up for what she had lost.

She was still day-dreaming when Jenny appeared at her elbow with a cup of tea.

"Oh! I didn't hear you go; I was miles away. Thank you, Jenny."

"It's nothing, miss, but I'll have to go now. I've got the stairs to do."

"How hard you work." Sara looked at the girl over the rim of her cup. "You make me feel ashamed."

"Ashamed?" Jenny was honestly puzzled. "Why should you be ashamed? You've done nothing wrong."

"Nothing wrong, no, but I'm so useless. All I do is to read and embroider. I take a walk with you or Aggie or Mercy Thorne; I drink tea and talk to Aunt Rachel's friends; I play the piano and sing to uncle's acquaintances. And that is all."

"But that's a lot to do, Miss. Not everyone can do those things, and what else could you do?"

"So much, if I had been given the chance. If I could have gone to school and college, like Oliver and Sidney, there is no knowing what I might have done. Instead, I had to stay and have lessons from poor old Amy Harris. I learned more from books than I did from her. Oh, Jenny, it is so hard to want to know everything, and to find there is no way of getting more than a smattering of real knowledge."

"Young ladies don't go away to school." Jenny was rather shocked at the notion. "And you do know a lot. I heard master say so not long ago. Proud of you, he was. I could tell."

"I don't know why he should be."

"I do." Jenny grinned and made for the door. "I must go, Miss Sara. Enjoy your tea."

Sara watched her go and sighed. Poor Jenny; she was as conventional as Uncle Arthur, seeing the place for genteel young ladies firmly in the home and nowhere else. Once she had tried to get Uncle Arthur to allow her to go away to school, but he had been as appalled as Jenny, chiding her for wanting to leave her family, and bidding her to listen carefully to Miss Harris's lessons.

Poor Amy Harris too. She had died the previous year of something which Aunt Rachel and Mercy spoke of in hushed whispers. Sara hoped she had not suffered too much, for she had been a kind creature for all her scholastic shortcomings.

Sara finished her tea and put the cup on the table outside the door for Jenny to pick up on her way downstairs. She stood in the hall for a moment, listening to the house drowsing. There were still whispers about that upper floor. Although the servants had changed over the years, the rumours hadn't. New lips mouthed old stories, and the stairs went on creaking at night.

Another hour or more before breakfast. Time to read a chapter or two of her book. Sara lifted her long skirts free of the ground and went upstairs, leaving the house to come to life slowly and to put on its face for another new day.

That afternoon at four o'clock tea was served in the sitting-room. Because it was Saturday the whole family was present, even Arthur Grey, looking mildly out of place amidst the wafer-thin sandwiches and delicate, hand-painted teacups. Two of Rachel's friends were there too, sitting close to her sofa so that they could exchange quiet asides with her when the topic of conversation grew really interesting.

Rachel had grown fatter still, almost bursting the seams of her *sang-de-boeuf* velvet, hiding the shelf of her bosom under a fringed shawl. Most of her looks had disappeared now, folded away between tucks of flesh. In a way Sara was relieved, although she knew it was wicked to be glad because someone had grown old, but now Rachel no longer looked like her sister Beth.

Oliver caught Sara's eye and winked. She returned a demure smile, trying not to laugh at their shared joke. Oliver was still regarded by the others as the fount of all knowledge, but nowadays he was too busy in the city to do more than keep a casual eye on his flock. Yet in the last month or two he had made it his business to find time to talk to Sara, and she was aware that their relationship had changed in some subtle, almost indefinable, way. Furthermore, once or twice Uncle Arthur had made a remark which sounded very much as though he were hinting at something more than cousinly friendship. Sara had been startled, for she had never thought of Oliver in that light. He was like a brother to her, dictatorial but protective, always there to lean on if necessary. He was very good-looking, his excellent education sharpening his natural intelligence. Oliver would go far, particularly now that charm had replaced boyish malice.

They heard the faint tinkle of the front-door bell, ignoring it until Aggie appeared with a young man, bobbing to Rachel who had raised her eyebrows in frosty enquiry.

"Well?"

Aggie had no time to answer, for Mercy Thorne had risen from her seat and was coming forward, her face almost animated for once as she held out her hand.

"Matthew! Dear boy, how glad I am to see you."

She braved the wordless anger of Rachel and her friends, drawing the newcomer to the sofa to be assessed.

"Rachel, this is my nephew, Matthew Compton; my sister's boy. You will remember that I have spoken of him."

"No." Rachel's basilisk stare emphasised the denial as she took stock of the intruder. "No, I do not recall a mention of him."

Mercy flushed, her momentary happiness gone. Rachel could not have made it plainer that she resented her housekeeper's relations being introduced into her cosy tea-time tête-à-tête. In was inherent in every forbidding line of her face, and in the chill of her voice.

"Well, never mind." Grey came to the rescue quickly, seeing the doubt in the young man. "He's here now, so let us get to know him. After all, if he is Mercy's nephew, he must be related to me too."

"Very distantly, Arthur." Rachel was repressive. "I hardly

think...."

Arthur took no notice, shaking Compton by the hand, introducing him to the family and to Rachel's friends.

Rebecca took careful stock of Matthew Compton when it was her turn to bid him welcome. He had fair hair, curled over a well-shaped head, steady grey eyes and a strong jaw. His clothes were not expensive but they were neatly pressed, his linen immaculate. When he smiled, his teeth were white and strong, and he had a dimple in each cheek. Rebecca's eyes were bright as she took his hand, venturing the slightest pressure on his fingers to let him know she was pleased to see him whatever Mama had to say. His smile deepened as he bowed over her hand, passing on to Henrietta and finally to Sara.

When Sara saw his face she felt a sudden jolt. She was used to admiration, and had not had her head turned by it. Uncle Arthur's friends were always ready with their praise, but she felt no particular elation at their words. Their homage had been conventional. A twinkle in the eye, a quick nod of approval, an extra warm smile; nothing more. Matthew Compton was looking at her as if he were about to take her in his arms, and she almost shrank back in her chair, half-afraid of such naked emotion. Then the moment was gone, and he had passed on to Sidney.

Although the small encounter had been so brief, it had been well-noted by all present. Arthur Grey was frowning. He didn't remember the boy, for all that Mercy said he was her nephew. Still, she ought to know, of course, yet he hadn't liked the way Compton had looked at Sara. Too bold, by far; too intimate. He hoped Mercy wasn't going to make a habit of inviting him to the house. He didn't want any complications, for he'd already made up his mind about Sara's future, and Matthew Compton played no part in his plans.

Oliver had also seen Compton's face and was silently grinding his teeth. Damned insolent of Mercy Thorne to bring the man here in the first place; appalling bad taste for him to stare at Sara as if he were about to eat her up. He moved a step or two so that he was behind Sara's chair, laying one hand lightly on her shoulder to establish something which Compton had better understand pretty quickly.

Rebecca's eyes were dark with rage. She had felt instantly attracted to Matthew, and he had certainly returned the pressure of her fingers. He had been interested, that is, until he had seen Sara. She moved her head slightly so she could watch her cousin, feeling something very like pain as she considered the near-perfect profile and the slim, beautiful figure in sea-green silk.

Henrietta poured her mother another cup of tea, her face impassive. Since it was clear that she would never marry, for who would want to marry anyone with so little claim to beauty as she, she had cast herself in the role of Rachel's guardian. Mercy Thorne spent most of her time running the house these days, and Rachel needed more attention, constantly demanding this and that, petulant and fractious as she watched her husband drift further and further away from her. She was glad enough to have Henrietta always at her side; it gave her a sense of security. Henrietta shot a hard look at Sara. She hoped her cousin was not going to ruffle the calm waters of the household by encouraging Matthew Compton. He was obviously drawn to Sara, but he must be made to see straight away that there was no place for him at No. 11, Candle Square.

"What do you do, m'boy?"

Arthur Grey shrugged off his disquiet. He was being unnecessarily cautious. After all, the lad had only come to call on his aunt, nothing more.

"I'm articled to a solicitor, sir, in Lincoln's Inn."

"Are you now?"

Arthur felt a twinge of surprise. He had expected something else, and he gave Compton a keener look.

"An honourable profession. I wish you well."

"Thank you. I expect to succeed. After all, it is up to us

to shape our lives, is it not?"

"Eh? Oh yes, I suppose so."

"Matthew is very clever." Mercy's thin face still bore the stain of embarrassment. "Everyone says so. And he's very musical too."

"Come, aunt, you will make me blush." Matthew grinned charmingly. "Aunt Mercy would set me up higher than I deserve, but I do love music, it is true. I am looking forward to the concert at Cranley Hall next week." He paused, giving Sara a quick look. "Sir, I suppose it would not be possible for Miss Lessingham to join me, and, of course, her cousins too. It is on Thursday at eight o'clock."

Grey's lips tightened, but he was saved the bother of finding an acceptable excuse when Rachel said coldly:

"It is quite out of the question, Mr... Mr... er... Compton. My niece does not go to concerts with strangers. Besides, the Brockleys are coming to dinner."

"I am not a stranger, Mrs. Grey." Compton was unmoved by the crushing rebuff. "I am Mercy's nephew. He went over to Rachel, smiling down at her, daring her to challenge his statement. "But, of course, if you have guests, that is different. I shall hope that on another occasion it may be possible. And now I must go. Thank you for the tea; it was most refreshing."

He bowed his farewells, walking to the door with Mercy Thorne, patting her arm encouragingly.

"Well, really!"

Rachel lay back against the velvet cushions and reached for her smelling-salts. She had expected to squash the impudent gate-crasher with one well-timed rebuke, but instead he had almost laughed at her protests, leaving with his head held high, a promise to return on his lips.

"Such insolence."

"I have never heard of such a thing."

Grey let Rachel and her friends commence their strictures, his mind winging off to other things, but he could not quite rid himself of the remembrance of Compton's self-assurance which lay like a small burr within him, disturbing his peace of mind.

When tea was over and the guests had gone, he said casually:

"Well, Sara, it seems that you have made a conquest."

He did not smile, and Sara could see that he was uneasy.

"Oh, hardly that, uncle. He meant no harm."

"No harm, perhaps, but...."

"I hope Mercy won't bring him here again." Oliver was terse. "Father, you should speak to her. After all, she is only a ser...."

He broke off as he met his father's eye. It was so easy to forget that Mercy was his father's distant cousin. No one had thought of her in that light for years, until Compton had reminded them of the fact.

"I'm sorry. I mean that...."

"Yes, I know." Grey was soothing, for his mind was at one with his son's on this issue. "I doubt that he'll come again, and Sara has other things to think about, haven't you, m'dear?" He smiled almost roguishly. "No need for you to miss the concert, if you want to go. Oliver can take you. Mercy had better go along as well I suppose."

He nodded benignly at them and moved off, and the incident was closed. Sara went into the drawing-room with the others and began to sew a cover for a footstool. It was a totally useless piece of work, but there was nothing else to do until it was time to dress for dinner.

Poor Mercy. Her temerity had certainly set the cat amongst the pigeons, and Sara had no doubt that she would feel the lash of Aunt Rachel's tongue when they were next alone. But Uncle Arthur hadn't been pleased either, nor had Oliver. They had closed about her protectively, angry because Compton had smiled at her; outraged because he had invited her to a concert. It was clear that they were both serious about those hints, and that before long she would be called upon to make a decision. She concealed her worry, keeping her head bent over her work. It would be very difficult; she could see that. There was no easy way to tell Arthur Grey that she did not want to marry his son; no way of rejecting Oliver without hurting him. But she would have to find some solution, no matter how hard it was. She was very fond of Oliver, but she could not marry him, and that was that.

At two o'clock in the morning Sara woke from the worst nightmare she had had for years. She was screaming aloud, aware of it as the black dread of the dream fell away like strands of cobwebs, fighting to push back the bedclothes.

Suddenly there were lights as candles bobbed in through the door, and there were Henrietta, Mercy and Rebecca, followed closely by Arthur Grey and a worried Oliver.

"Sara! What is it? Whatever is wrong?"

Mercy stood her candle on the bedside table, pulling the blankets into place, taking Sara's shaking hand in hers.

"Child, you're shivering. Are you cold? What is the matter?"

"I was dreaming." Sara lay back against the pillows, only half-aware of the circle of concerned faces round her. "It was a bad dream."

"Is that all?" Rebecca was cross, pulling her peignoir tighter about her. "We thought someone was murdering you, you made such a noise."

"I'm sorry. I didn't mean to disturb you all. I . . . I . . . couldn't help it."

"Of course you couldn't." Oliver was short. "Can you remember what you dreamed? Sometimes it helps to talk about it."

"I . . . I . . . yes, I can remember. It is always the same dream."

"You have had this nightmare before?" Grey pursed his lips. "Better tell us, m'dear."

"It was the fire. I dreamt I was home again . . . that is . . . at my father's house. We were all there, father, mother and me. Then it grew dark, and I could hear something roaring, and I could see my mother's face, and then there was . . . no! No, no, I don't want to talk about it any more."

"I think we must."

Arthur settled himself heavily on the side of the bed and took her hand, patting it gently.

"I really think we must talk of it, Sara. It is time you knew the truth. Someone will tell you one day, that's certain, and it's better that you should learn it from your own family than from strangers. Besides, perhaps these dreams come because you have not been made to face the truth."

Sara looked up abruptly, aware of a note in her uncle's voice she had not heard before.

"The truth? I don't understand. What truth? About the fire, do you mean? But I know about that. My mother and father were killed."

"Yes, yes, but there was more to it than that."

He was very grave, squeezing her fingers between his as if to reassure her.

"More? Uncle, I don't understand. What more could there be?"

"It is not easy to tell you. I had hoped it wouldn't be necessary, but I can see I was wrong about that."

"Please! Uncle! What are you talking about?"

"The fire, Sara; the fire."

"What about it?"

"Fires have to start somehow you know. They don't begin by themselves."

"I know, I know! What of it?"

He hesitated a moment longer. Then he said slowly:

"When they found you, Sara, you had a box of matches in your hand. Sometimes you used to walk in your sleep. Did you know that?"

Sara shook her head numbly. That the fire had started at all was bad enough; that she had been responsible for it was more than the mind could support. She was vaguely aware of the faces growing closer. Henrietta's expressionless as ever; Oliver's stricken; Mercy's startled; Rebecca's expectant, a trace of a smile on her lips.

"You were too young to know, of course; about the sleep-walking I mean." Grey went on quickly. "Too young to understand what it was all about. No one blamed you, my dear, and you mustn't blame yourself now. It was just a tragic accident."

"I killed them?" Sara got the words out at last. "I killed my own mother and father?"

"Not knowingly." Grey was sombre. "You mustn't think of it like that. Who knows what tricks the mind can play if it becomes unbal. . . . No, you mustn't think of it that way. I want you to put this out of your mind. Now that you know the truth I am sure things will be different. The dreams won't come back, now we've had this talk. Mercy, get the gel a glass of hot milk."

When they had all gone and Sara was alone, she sat up in bed and lit the candle again. The milk had warmed her and made her feel drowsy, but there was something to consider before sleep could come.

It had been a shattering revelation. Uncle Arthur's words had been like a sword-thrust, and yet a second after they had been uttered she knew they had the ring of truth about them. She had always known that there was something she ought to have remembered about that night; something which she had always shied away from whenever she grew near to it. And now she knew. Arthur had said that when the mind became unbalanced, it played tricks. He hadn't quite finished the word, but everyone present had understood. They had been so kind; Arthur, Oliver, Henrietta and Mercy. Rebecca had not bent to kiss her as the others had done, but perhaps even she was sorry for her unfortunate cousin.

Sara gritted her teeth and made a vow. It was done. It had happened many years ago when she had been a child. Deadly though the burden was, it would have to be carried through life, and life must go on in spite of it.

She blew out the candle and turned resolutely on her side,

forcing her eyelids shut and swearing to herself most fervently that she would not dream again that night.

By late October, Sara Lessingham had come to terms with life again. No one had mentioned by word or glance the tale which Arthur Grey had had to tell, and Sara was determinedly cheerful as she went about her everyday tasks, almost gay as she closed the door of her mind upon the past.

Much to the consternation and annoyance of Arthur and Rachel Grey, Matthew Compton had called several times during the month. It was difficult, if not impossible, actually to refuse him entry. After all, as Mercy Thorne had said, he was her nephew. Grudgingly they had received him at tea; and had once been forced to offer him luncheon. He seemed totally oblivious to their disapproval, charming and courteous to Rachel and the girls, obviously greatly attracted to Sara, to whom he paid special attention.

In normal circumstances, Sara would probably have avoided him. She could see that her aunt and uncle were not pleased to have him there, and she would not have encouraged him had things been as usual. As it was, she was glad to see a new face; someone who didn't know what had happened ten years ago. She did not respond too openly, of course, but neither did she rebuff him, and now and then she caught Uncle Arthur looking at her, his face very serious.

No one was quite sure how Matthew had managed to get himself invited to the party which was held in the last week of October. Rachel blamed Arthur, and Arthur blamed Mercy Thorne, and Oliver blamed all of them.

"I don't think you ought to speak to him," he said to Sara on the morning of the party. "The man's a bounder, or he wouldn't come here so often. He must know he's not wanted."

"Mercy likes to see him." Sara was evasive. She did not want to have to grapple with the reason behind Oliver's anger. "He does no harm."

"Doesn't he?" Oliver was almost curt. "He does no good,

at any rate. It's easy to see what he feels about you, Sara. You shouldn't encourage him."

"Oliver, I don't." She would not meet his eye. "I just cannot ignore him if he speaks to me. It would hurt Mercy."

"Damn Mercy!"

"Oliver!"

"I'm sorry." He was instantly contrite. "I forget myself when I think about Compton. Promise me you won't. . . ."

"Won't what?"

"Well . . . pay any attention to him to-night."

"I can't be rude."

"All right, but keep him at arm's length."

By six o'clock that evening the fog which had been threatening all day closed in. The houses on the opposite side of the Square slowly disappeared in its embracing arms, and gas-lights faded to mere blobs of hazy light.

Despite the inclement weather, most of the guests had arrived by seven, and at eight there was a splendid buffet supper served in the dining-room. Regardless of her aches and pains, Mrs. Tamworth had surpassed herself, and, with the aid of Aggie Lowther, Jenny and a girl hired for the night, had prepared a spread which satisfied even Aunt Rachel, who had risen from her sofa long enough to make a close inspection of the tables.

There were two long boards, covered with fair linen cloths, shining with sparkling glass and silver, and ornate épergnes in the centre of each table piled high with fruit and decorated with flowers. There were dishes of tongue, boiled and roast chicken, garnished ham, Tipsy Cake, jellies, meringues, iced biscuits and a dozen other delicacies.

"You look beautiful, Sara." Oliver whispered between welcoming one guest and the next. "You won't forget what I said, will you?"

Sara nodded absently. She wore a gown of eau-de-nil crêpe-de-chine, off the shoulders and tight round her slender waist. The skirt was an extravagance of pleats and frills, lifted high in a ruche behind, and flat across the stomach. It had cost a great deal of money and she had been embarrassed when Uncle Arthur had bought it for her, protesting that she did not need so many new clothes, and could manage with what she had. He had given his deep, rich laugh and patted her on the cheek.

"Not only yourself you have to please," he had said, and winked. "Must make the best of yourself now."

"Sara! Did you hear what I said?"

She started guiltily.

"Yes, yes. Oh yes, Oliver, I heard. I promise I will only say good-evening to Matthew, nothing else."

Then more guests arrived and she became separated from Oliver, talking to many people as the evening wore on, faithful to her promise when she encounterd Matthew Compton and murmured no more than a perfunctory greeting.

It was ten o'clock when the news of the tragedy came. As the hired footman approached Arthur Grey, no one paid attention to the fact, despite the ashen quality of the man's face and the way in which his mouth was working. They were too busy talking and drinking their wine; safe and warm and content, shut off from the fog outside.

"What!"

Grey's brows met in a quick frown and he put his glass down on a nearby table.

"What's that you say, man? Someone has fallen into the area? Are you sure?"

"Certain, sir. One of the boys went out there to see if the fog was lifting, and tripped over him."

"Well, who is it? Where is he now? Is he hurt?"

Grey was moving to the door, followed by the footman.

"What is it, uncle?"

Sara saw the look on Arthur Grey's face, and felt a hand squeeze her heart.

"Nothing, my dear, nothing. Stay here. Too cold for you outside."

He did not wait to hear her response, unaware in his haste that she was following.

Sara felt the fog slide over her like an icy mantle, stumbling as she made her way down the front steps and groped along the railings.

"Who left this gate open?"

She could hear Grey's irritable question and followed his voice.

"I don't know, sir. It wasn't open earlier."

"Damned carelessness. No wonder someone has fallen. Missed his way in the fog, of course. Here, give me a light."

There was silence for a moment as Sara began to descend the iron steps, and she was taken completely unawares when Arthur Grey let out a sharp sound somewhere between a scream and a moan.

"Uncle! What is it! Uncle Arthur, what is wrong?"

"Oh God!" Grey was on his knees, barely visible until Sara reached his side. He was holding a slack form in his arms, tight against his breast, tears starting from his eyes. "Oh my God, my God! Oliver!"

"Oliver?"

Sara's legs gave way and she sank down beside her uncle, putting out a tentative hand to touch his arm.

"Uncle, is Oliver . . . hurt? What has happened to him?"

Grey did not reply, but the servant loomed out of the fog and got her to her feet.

"Come inside, miss. This is no place for you now."

"But Oliver . . . my cousin. I can't go in yet. I must know what has happened. I have got to help him."

"Can't do that, miss; he's dead. Come along in. Here, mind how you go."

The next hour was utter confusion. Somehow the guests were speeded on their way, and the family had made for the sitting-room, where the servants had kept the fire piled high in the grate. Aggie and Jenny brought in trays of hot tea doctored with brandy, and Mercy produced a fresh bottle of smelling-salts for Rachel.

At first they did not say much. They sat in a semi-circle

round the fire, drinking their tea and keeping their grief to themselves, except for Rachel who was sobbing openly, murmuring her son's name under her breath.

Finally, Henrietta said slowly :

"Why was he out there, do you suppose?"

Sidney cleared his throat. He was the eldest male now, after his father. He had to take Oliver's place, but it wouldn't be easy.

"He was probably going out to meet one of the guests."

"But they would come up the front steps."

"He may have gone down to the pavement and then missed his way."

"Perhaps he wanted to see if the fog had lifted, like the boy who found him."

They made their points, their voices ragged with emotion. Arthur Grey sat near to his wife, silent in the face of the overwhelming blow which fate had dealt him. He could not quite believe it yet. Oliver, his first-born, his beloved son; lying at the foot of the area steps, his neck broken.

He did not even have enough spirit left in him to protest when Matthew Compton came to ask if there was anything he could do. The others shook their heads, and Mercy gave her nephew a cup of tea.

"I saw him outside earlier on."

They all turned their heads to look at Matthew, as if they were pulled by a single string.

"You saw him?" Henrietta was sharp. "When? What was he doing out there?"

"I don't know. Talking to someone on the pavement, I think. I caught a glimpse of him and then heard voices. Couldn't see much because of the fog."

"What were you doing there?" Henrietta's voice was tart with suspicion. "Why did you go outside?"

"I was dancing with one of your guests. She wanted to know if her carriage had arrived and asked me to call the footman. I couldn't find him; I suppose he was busy. She told me where the carriage would be waiting, and so I went to see for myself."

"Who was she?"

"I've no idea." Compton shrugged his regrets. "There were so many here, I could not remember all the names. Sir?" He went over to Arthur and lowered his voice. "Is there anything I can do?"

Grey looked at Matthew for a long minute. Then he shook his head, and after a suitable interval Compton left, with the tearful Mercy at his side.

"I cannot bear it; I cannot bear it!"

Rachel's wail was ugly, her eyes puffed and red.

"Henrietta." Grey roused himself from his torment. "Take your mother upstairs. Rebecca, help her."

"She should see a doctor, father."

"He won't come out on a night like this, and a doctor won't help her, or me either. Oliver is dead. Oh dear God; Oliver is dead."

But the next morning the doctor came and the police returned too. The police were solicitous and helpful, full of sympathy, but they could not add to what was already known despite the enquiries which they had been making. Oliver Grey had gone out of the house on the night before, for what reason no one could tell. He was seen and heard at about nine o'clock. At ten o'clock he had been found dead.

There was not the slightest suspicion of foul play. It was clearly an accident, or so the inspector assured Arthur Grey. Oliver had missed his footing and fallen through the open gate leading down to the area. There was nothing further to be done, save to make the funeral arrangements.

When Oliver had been laid to rest amidst a flurry of black-plumed horses and heavily-scented lilies, the household did its best to settle back to its normal routine.

Rachel had finally stopped weeping, and was receiving a stream of curious and excited friends, each anxious to know the exact details of what had happened. Grey had aged suddenly. He hardly mentioned Oliver's name, turning to Sidney instead for support, talking of taking him into the firm at once, despite the fact that it would mean cutting short the college education which had been so near and dear to his heart.

He even tolerated Matthew Compton's presence, or at least made no outward objection when he called, shutting himself up in his study when he was not at his office in the city.

Sara was just beginning to recover from the jarring sorrow of Oliver's death when her world was once more turned upside down. It happened at breakfast-time, early in November.

Mercy was pouring coffee, her old self again, grief hidden behind the waxen mask. She looked up as Rebecca came in, slightly flushed as if something was exciting her.

"You are late, Rebecca." Grey frowned. "You know how I hate unpunctuality. Why don't you get up when Mercy calls you?"

"I am sorry, father." She wasn't. She was smiling as she accepted her cup and began to stir in some sugar. "I was up in good time, but I found I had no clean handkerchiefs and so I went to Sara's room to borrow one."

Sara felt something tremble along her spine. The words were innocent enough, but the look in Rebecca's eyes wasn't.

"You didn't mind, Sara, did you?"

"No . . . no."

"Oh good." Rebecca buttered her toast carefully. "Sara."

"Yes?"

"Why do you keep a box of matches in your handkerchief sachet?"

Sara's face grew pale and everyone stopped eating to stare at her.

"A . . . box of matches? But I don't."

"There's one there now." Rebecca licked a crumb from her lips. "I have just seen it with my own two eyes. You're not going to set fire to this house too, are you?"

There was a stunned silence; then Grey laid down his knife and fork and said slowly:

"Sara; after breakfast I would like to see you in the study. There are things we must talk about."

THREE

Sara thought a lot about that interview. She was still considering it two days later when she and Arthur Grey were clipping along at a good pace in the brougham towards Mile End. She had not really wanted to go with him, but it had been hard to refuse. A former cook, Mrs. Bosey, whom Sara remembered vaguely, was in an institution there. Drink had been her ruin, so Aunt Rachel had said, and once a year Grey felt it his duty to visit her and take her a parcel of comforts. Normally Henrietta went with her father, but to-day she was busy with Rachel. Rebecca had a music lesson and Mercy Thorne was preparing for a dinner party. It was good of Uncle Arthur to bother with such a mission when he had so much to do; she was churlish even to have considered making an excuse.

She hardly saw the crowded East End streets with their press of people, shouting vendors thrusting their wares noisily under the noses of passers-by.

It was growing dark, and the gas-lamps had already been lit, concealing some of the poverty, but the grubby tapestry of human misery rushing by her on every side was not strong enough to interrupt Sara's own thoughts. Uncle Arthur had been very kind that morning two days ago. He had not scolded her because Rebecca said she had found matches in the handkerchief sachet; indeed, he had hardly mentioned the incident. Instead, he had spoken of her future, gravely but with gentleness.

"I had hoped you and Oliver would marry," he had said, and his voice had shaken slightly. He did not often mention Oliver's name now. "But that . . . that cannot be, but there is Sidney."

He had ignored her startled look.

"He is young, of course, but a responsible boy, and he is very fond of you."

She had tried to protest that she did not want to marry anyone, least of all Sidney. The suggestion was quite absurd, and she had tried to tell Grey so, but he had not been listening.

"You need someone to care for you, Sara. I shall not always be here to do that, and you must marry if you are to have a normal life. If you don't, you may have relapses and even need treatment, and we don't want that, do we?"

"Treatment?"

She knew that she had said the word too loudly, but Uncle Arthur had not seemed to notice.

"But there's no need to dwell on that, is there? Marriage, that's what you need. A home to run and children to bring up. Plenty to keep you busy. Sidney has good prospects, you know, and he is devoted to you. His health is better too nowadays."

She had been firm, once she had got her breath back. It was an impossible proposal and she had had to make Grey see that straight away.

"Uncle, I am not ready to marry yet." She had sat up straight in her chair, her hands clenched together. "You must not think I do not appreciate your concern, but I am not ready for this. Besides, Sidney...."

"Yes?"

His eyes had slid to hers, holding them for a moment.

"Sidney is . . . is like my brother. I couldn't marry him."

"Too early to make a decision yet, my dear." Arthur had remained unperturbed by her dogmatic refusal. "Think about it, and you'll come to see that I am right. Only thinking of you, Sara, and what is best for you in the circumstances."

"Here we are, m'dear."

Sara came back to the present with a bump, finding the carriage had stopped and the coachman was opening the door.

She got out reluctantly, staring up at the gaunt, shabby building with bars protecting its narrow windows. Over the door she could see the faded lettering: "Thomlins' Charity Home for the Poor and Insane", and felt her heart sink. She would have liked to have got into the brougham again, ordering the coachman to drive off anywhere, as long as it was away from there, but then there was no time left for the door was opening and a heavy-set woman welcoming them in.

It was icy cold inside; even colder than in the streets. The corridors along which they walked had been cleaned that day, for Sara could still smell the disinfectant, but the walls were pitted with dirt, the ceiling overhead a harbour for spiders. Further on they met two women sweeping the floor. They wore shapeless sack-like garments, with old shawls round their shoulders. Then others appeared. A man with long hair and blank eyes who giggled incessantly; another youth, thin as a bone, twitching with epilepsy; a girl, no more than twelve, who had somehow managed to retain rosy cheeks and bright eyes, but who dribbled like an infant.

Sara felt sick. Suddenly she was ashamed of her warm mohair gown with its careful rows of silver buttons and swathe of silk on the skirt; the Balmoral mantle with wide sleeves; the neat black hat with the tiny rolled brim and plume of ostrich feathers. She was out of place. A walking taunt to the unfortunate creatures who had barely enough clothing to make them decent, never mind to keep the chill from their flesh.

They came to a square hall where fifty or so of the inmates were eating. Long wooden tables and forms; just sufficient light for them to see the tin mugs of weak tea and dishes of watery stew.

"Here we are." The woman had turned off into another corridor and was stopping to unlock a door. "Have to keep these shut up, sir. Never know what they'd get up to if we let them roam. You'll find Bosey well enough. Over in the corner, there."

Sara fought down the retching as the smell hit them. She had never known anything like it before, recoiling as she picked her way carefully after Grey, wary lest some of the bundles on the floor should be of human origin.

There were eight people in the room, all crouched on straw mattresses. One gas lamp lit the place.

Mrs. Bosey, or what was left of her, had hunched herself up into a small heap against the wall. Her loose grey hair had not been washed for months and straggled over her shoulders in dirty strands. Her face was lined with age and pain, her mouth distorted in misery.

"Well, Mrs. Bosey, and how are you?"

Grey was booming, trying not to let his disgust shew.

"See, we've brought you a few things. Some cakes and biscuits; fruit and chocolate too."

He put the wicker basket down gingerly, backing away as the woman made a grab for it.

She was mumbling something as she searched feverishly under the white cloth, angry with him as her dilated eyes met his. Then she began to shout and whine, hitting herself with clenched hands, tearing at her own face with nails as long as talons.

"Uncle! What is it?"

"Don't know, m'dear. She wants something, but what I don't know. Here, Mrs. Bosey, have some of this. Best cherry cake; try some."

Mrs. Bosey started to laugh, and the sound froze the blood in Sara's veins. Then the woman struggled to her feet and made for them, and in another second had flung herself at Grey. The shouting and noise brought their guide back in a hurry, and she thrust her way through the door and hauled Mrs. Bosey off her startled visitor.

She had no time to be gentle. Sara watched with horror as she struck the raving woman across the head, knocking her senseless against the wall, kicking her back on to her mattress so that she was no longer under their feet.

"Only way to deal with them," said the wardress as she

locked the door behind them. "No time for anything else. She'd have 'ad yer eyes out, sir, if I 'adn't come in when I did."

Grey nodded, giving Sara a troubled look.

"She seemed to want something. We could not understand what it was she needed."

"Gin." The woman was leading them back to the entrance hall. "That's easy enough, sir—gin. Never 'appy unless she can get a nip, though she don't get much in 'ere, I can tell you."

She was not sitting in judgment on Mrs. Bosey; merely stating a fact. She had a hundred men and women to look after, and the cravings of one old drunkard were of no significance.

"It is a terrible place." Sara waited until they were safely back in the brougham before she spoke. "Uncle, it is dreadful."

"Yes, my dear, I'm afraid it is. They are all like that."

"They?"

"The workhouses, especially those which take the insane. It's like this every year. Sometimes I think I won't come again, but then I remember that it's my duty."

"She doesn't know you."

"No, she's forgotten, but we mustn't forget her. She is one of life's unfortunates. There's no place left in the world for her now; only at Thomlins'."

"It was so . . . so dark and cold and cheerless."

"The mad don't notice these things."

"They were so hungry too."

He cleared his throat.

"They do the best they can; the authorities, I mean. I shouldn't have brought you, Sara; it was thoughtless of me. Henrietta has grown used to it, of course, but I should have known that it would upset you."

Sara shivered. She thought she heard an odd note in Grey's voice which she did not want to analyse. Of course it was right that Grey should not forget his old employees, even if they had grown crazy with overwork and drink, but why had he wanted her to come with him?

She stole a look at Grey's face. Could he have been trying to shew her what happened to people whose minds no longer functioned normally? Did he really think that she had hidden those matches and was planning to use them? No, Uncle Arthur would not be so cruel. He had always been kind and considerate, yet more than once he had pressed her to marry, first Oliver and now Sidney. He could trust his own sons to care for his niece.

She felt a moment of rebellion. It was quite ridiculous. She had not put the matches there. She had no idea how they had come to be in her drawer, unless someone had put them there as a joke. But who would be so wicked? Rebecca? Henrietta? Aggie? Certainly not Jenny.

Then the spurt of anger died. How could she be absolutely sure that she hadn't hidden them there herself? Uncle had said that as a child she had walked in her sleep. Had she done that again? She had had matches once before; Uncle Arthur had said so. They had found her with them, after the fire.

"You look tired." Grey tucked the rug firmly about her knees. "I was a fool to bring you. Forgive me, my dear."

She murmured something, smiling at him vaguely, not yet done with her doubts.

Did other people dream as she did? They were not ordinary dreams. If she were really normal, would she scream herself awake at the sights she saw when she slept? She closed her eyes, but all she could see was the face of Mrs. Bosey, contorted, frantic, and quite, quite mad.

The next morning Sara's head ached and she felt an odd lethargy as she made her way to the morning-room. Aunt Rachel was by herself, her sofa pulled up close to the fire, making a list of guests for a dinner party.

"I cannot think why Henrietta is taking so long with cook." Rachel was irritable, for she hated to be alone. "She has been downstairs for half an hour or more. It's Mercy's fault, of course. Why she needed two hours off, I cannot think. So selfish. She has no thought for me at all. Sara, you will have to go."

"Yes, aunt." Sara was only half-aware of the stream of complaints, wondering what Rachel would say if she could see Thomlins' Charity Home. "What is it you want?"

"The blue address book; it must be in your uncle's study. He borrowed it the other day. Go and get it for me, child. How can I finish this list unless I have it?"

"Where shall I find it?"

Rachel looked at her in exasperation.

"In the desk. Really, Sara, you might pay attention to me when I am talking to you. In the desk, of course, and don't be too long."

Sara flushed and hurried away, feeling like an intruder as she made her way to the study. The room was cold, for the fire would not be lit until after lunch, and there was a smell of beeswax from Jenny's diligent polishing of the leather chairs and walnut desk. Sara opened one drawer and then another, the feeling of guilt increasing. She hoped her uncle would not find out that she had been there, even at Aunt Rachel's request. She was about to close the third drawer when the envelope caught her attention. It was long, and the paper had yellowed with age, but it was the superscription which held her transfixed as slowly she picked it up and stared at it. 'Sara Lessingham'. At first she thought her eyes were playing tricks on her, but there was no mistake; it was addressed to her. She wondered how long it had lain in the drawer, and why Uncle Arthur had not given it to her. She turned it over, seeing that the flap was not securely sealed, and in another second she had pulled out the sheet of paper and was reading it.

It was from her grandfather and bore a date nine years before; just a month or two before he died.

" 'My dearest Sara', it began, and she felt a flicker of surprise. Had he been so fond of her? He had not wanted her when her parents died, and she had heard very little of him after that. But the opening was warm and loving and she found an unexpected lump in her throat as she read on. 'If you should ever need help, and if I should no longer be there to offer you aid, go to my old friend Lord Westerbrook in Eaton Square. No matter what troubles you, he will listen with sympathy and do what he can to. . . .'

Sara bit her lip. There was no more, for the bottom of the page had been torn off. She searched in the envelope for the missing scrap, or another page, but there was nothing.

Quickly she slipped the sheet into the envelope and hid it at the back of the drawer. Why had her grandfather thought that she might want help? He knew that Uncle Arthur and Aunt Rachel had given her a good home, so why did he think she might have need of another's counsel? 'He will listen with sympathy'. An odd phrase. Why should she need sympathy? She stood alone in the study, her face wan. She did need sympathy, of course. Grandfather had been right. Had he known about the cause of the fire, and the sleep-walking?

Clearly he had, and had taken steps to provide her with a receptive ear for her troubles. But why had Uncle Arthur not shewn her the letter? Why had he hidden it away?

She found the address book and closed the study door behind her, the thought still nagging at her until she was back in the morning-room, helping Aunt Rachel with her list.

Then it struck her. Of course! Uncle Arthur would not want her to think that her grandfather considered her odd and likely to be in need of help. He would want to protect her from such a notion, wrapping her about with his love and kindness.

She would never tell him that she had seen the letter; how could she, since she had been prying into his desk? But she would not forget what her grandfather had said either. One day she might be glad to visit his friend and to see what he made of a young woman who dreamed bad dreams and hid boxes of matches amongst her handkerchiefs.

On the following Friday, Sara went shopping with Mercy Thorne and Jenny. She had recovered from the sight of Mrs. Bosey and her own morbid thoughts, and set out for Regent Street with a light heart.

Regent Street was the Mecca of all dedicated shoppers with a full purse. At eight o'clock it began to prepare itself for the day, removing its shutters and dressing its great plate-glass windows with the newest mantles and hats, bales of plush velvet, moiré silk, fluttering gauzes and laces, French gloves and trim leather boots.

By eleven o'clock it was thronged with carriages and people, all in their best finery, making an occasion of their shopping. Because it was a dark morning the gas-flares were alight, and everything seemed to have a special glitter as Sara and her companions made their way into Sawbridges to buy some pillow cases.

"Three dozen linen slips," said Mercy, consulting her list. "See that they are of the finest quality, and well-stitched."

"Yes, madam. Is there anything else?"

"Some sheets. Three pairs of linen for a double bed and four pairs of cotton, single size. Oh, and four pairs of cheap cotton too, for the servants. Have them sent to Mrs. Arthur Grey at 11, Candle Square."

That mundane chore over, they moved to Laceys where they bought some lavender water for Aunt Rachel and scented soap for Rebecca, and then on to Christals, where Sara used a good deal of her dress allowance to buy a length of honey-coloured taffeta for a new evening dress.

They had some hot chocolate in a small café which was wedged between a linen-draper's and a hatshop, Jenny's eyes round with wonder at the red plush seats and gilt tables. She was not often allowed to go on such expeditions and this was a special treat.

They came out into the dreary morning again, their senses battered by the noise of hansom cabs, the broughams, the omnibuses and the four-wheelers.

They waited on the kerb for a chance to cross the road, Mercy warning Jenny to mind her feet as a barouche, high-hung on its C-springs, whisked past them at a fast pace.

Afterwards, when Sara tried to recall exactly what had happened, she could only remember the confusion. She felt herself propelled forward with a sudden jerk, hearing Jenny's scream and Mercy's gasp of consternation. She saw the roadway leap up to meet her, conscious that there was a pair of hooves very nearly over her head, and that out of the corner of her eye she could see great wheels bearing down upon her.

Then she fainted, and the journey home was a mere blur. Propped up in bed two hours later, her ankle tightly bandaged and her bruised arm aching painfully, she tried to tell the others what had happened.

"Someone pushed me."

She knew her voice sounded high-pitched, and she forced herself to be calm as she saw the disbelief on their faces. Mercy was patient.

"Sara, don't be so foolish. Of course no one pushed you. You slipped."

"No! I felt someone push me."

Henrietta shook her head slightly, exchanging a significant look with Mercy.

"Who would do that?" She said it as if she were trying to humour a feeble-witted child. "You must be mistaken."

"I am not mistaken." Sara was pale, still shaken by the incident but determined not to give way. "You were not there, Henrietta."

"But I was." Mercy Thorne's expression left no one in any doubt of her opinion. "I would have seen anyone push you. It's your imagination. You slipped."

"Jenny!" Sara turned to the maid who had brought up a tray with tea and thinly-cut bread and butter. "Jenny, did you see who it was behind me?"

Jenny was near to tears. She had had a bad fright, and for a moment had thought Miss Sara had been killed. She could still feel herself shaking at the very thought of it.

"No, miss, I didn't. There were so many people."

"Of course there were, but none of them would want to hurt you, Sara. Now, drink your tea, and then have a sleep. Dr. Blackmore said you should rest. Put the whole thing out of your mind."

Mercy was done with the subject, ushering Henrietta and Jenny out of the room, leaving Sara to sip her tea and feel the tears trickle down her face.

It couldn't have been imagination. She had felt the hand in the small of her back, vicious and determined. If she had merely lost her footing, she would not have fallen with such violence into the roadway. There had been someone there, but who? Why should anyone want to injure her in such a way?

There was no answer to that. Sara lay back against the pillows and tried not to dwell on it, for it was an ugly thought. Better to accept the judgment of Mercy. Perhaps it had been an accident after all.

She slept until seven, when Jenny brought her dinner on a tray. Chicken soup, roast mutton with red currant jelly, and a compôte of pears. She wasn't hungry, but she forced herself to eat, because she did not want the others to think that she was sulking.

The evening seemed very long. She tried to read a book, but the words danced in front of her eyes, and the pain in her ankle distracted her. She was glad when the time came to settle down for the night.

When the gas-light was turned off, it was very dark. Sara's small room was on the second floor, at the other end of the house from the servants' quarters. A year or two before, she had been given the choice of sharing a larger room with Rebecca, or having one which lay near to the stairs leading to the top floor. Despite her dislike of the shadowed archway and the winding steps, she had chosen the single room. By day it was bright and cheerful, with a suite of painted wood and a gay coverlet of frilled muslin on the bed.

Now and then she heard the stairs, but she had almost grown used to the sound. Despite the servants' whispers, she did not believe in ghosts any more. Old houses often creaked at night as they settled down to sleep; it was no more than that.

She closed her eyes, determined to clear her mind of troubled thoughts, but sleep would not come. It seemed to her that she lay awake for hours.

Then she heard a faint noise and sat up, straining to identify it, her mouth growing dry as it was repeated. It was the stairs; there was no doubt about that. It was just as if someone were ascending slowly and carefully to the top floor, cautious, yet not lightly enough to prevent the treads from complaining as weight was put on them.

But who would go up to an empty floor in the early hours of the morning?

She was imagining things again; turning normal night murmurs into phantoms. She must pull herself together, or people really would begin to think that she was odd. Oddness was not many steps away from madness, and madness was Mrs. Bosey, locked away in Thomlins' Charity Home for the Poor and Insane.

With something near to despair, Sara buried her head in her pillow and began to pray.

On that same evening, Candace Martin sat in the bedroom of her smart little villa in St. John's Wood and considered her face carefully in a gilt-edged mirror on the dressing-table.

She was twenty-four years old and very beautiful. The mirror assured her of the fact as it reflected the heavy auburn hair piled up on the small, shapely head and the huge green eyes which slanted upwards at the corners. She had darkened her thick lashes with a mixture of Chinese ink and rose-water, and touched her mouth with carmine lip-salve. A trace of rouge on the cheek-bones and a suggestion of powder completed her toilet.

As she dabbed her ears and throat with perfume she looked about her with contentment. Every item of furniture had been chosen with loving care, down to the smallest crystal vase, ivory snuff-box and satin pin-cushion.

It was a calm, peaceful room, made for one person. Candace smiled to herself. Somewhere hidden beneath the clinging peignoir of crêpe-de-chine, Jane Briggs lay buried. Candace thought about her sometimes; a ragged child who had lived in Meggs Yard in squalor and near-starvation.

She had not remained a child for very long, of course; Mrs. Letchworth had seen to that. She looked back now and then to that evening, remembering the short stout man who had looked at her hungrily. Although she had been so ignorant, the night had not been an unsuccessful one. She had found it amazingly easy to make love, almost enjoying it towards the end. The man had been satisfied, and so had Mrs. Letchworth.

After that, there had been no looking back. Jane had remained with Mrs. Letchworth for a year, but then she had begun to realise that she was being made use of, and that the wealthy men who came furtively to the house were paying handsomely for what they got, but that she, Jane, received no more than a few new clothes and three meals a day.

When she ran away, she changed her name. She was tired of Jane Briggs and her history, and wanted no more of her. For a while she worked in a milliner's shop, but at nights, she would go to the Haymarket to watch the *demi-monde* go by, and eventually she was picked up by an actor who had been moved by her slender figure and exquisite face. She stayed with him for two years, comparatively happy as she learned something of acting and a lot about pleasing men. When she was eighteen she had her first stroke of good fortune. One night, when the play was done, there was a man waiting for her at the stage door. He was an industrialist and very generous, and he had set her up in a small house in Fulham, visiting her twice a week, not enquiring too closely about what she did on the remaining nights.

Candace saved her money carefully, allowing her new protector to ply her with clothes, perfume and modest jewels, waiting until she had sufficient from him, and from the other men she entertained, to move to a more salubrious district. From Fulham she went to the edge of Kensington and then to the outskirts of Hampstead. When she was twenty-two she had enough to buy the villa in St. John's Wood.

She had quite a lot in the bank now, besides the villa and her own neat little barouche. Her wardrobe was full of expensive clothes, and she had different jewels to wear on each night of the week.

She thought she had been entirely satisfied with her lot until she met Blaise, but then she had realised that her life had been empty, shallow and without savour, for it had also been devoid of love. Love had not entered into Candace's scheme of things until she met him. She had a measure of fondness for some of those who visited her, but she had kept her head cool and her heart inviolate.

With Blaise it was different. She would have liked to have been with him every minute of the day and night, but she knew this was not possible. He was a leader of the fashionable set, his life fully occupied with the business of riding, hunting, dining, and gambling. He came to visit her perhaps twice a week, sometimes less. She found that she was growing jealous of the other, unknown, women with whom he spent the rest of his time, hating them silently, wishing that they were dead.

Now and then she dreamed of marriage. Others of her kind had managed to shake off their humble beginnings and dubious backgrounds in order to marry into the aristocracy. If they could do it, so could she. She had never mentioned the matter to Blaise, of course, for that might have frightened him away, but she nursed the possibility close to her heart, and thought about him as she undressed for the gratification of her customers.

She looked up as her maid came in with a cup of tea. Bessie

Poke was forty, plump, and good-natured. She had been on the streets herself, unsuccessful and near to starving when Candace had found her. She was very proud of her mistress, keeping her home spotless and shining for her, fussing and worrying over her in case she did not eat properly or get enough sleep when the long nights were over.

"Are you going out?"

Candace nodded and took the tea with a smile of thanks. "Yes, in a while. I'm having an early supper with a friend. Then perhaps I'll go on to Evans' Supper Rooms, or to the Argyll."

"Is he coming to-night?"

There was no need for Bessie to mention the name; Candace knew only too well whom she meant.

"No, not to-night." Candace kept her voice light. She did not want Bessie to hear the sick disappointment in it. She had hoped Blaise would come, but he had sent a message. Perhaps to-morrow, or the next day, he had said. She must not let her sorrow shew, for that would be an admission of her weakness. "Get out the lemon satin, will you, and tell John I shall want the carriage in half an hour."

Bessie Poke saw the look on her face and hurried off, and an hour later Candace was being shewn into the salon of one of the most notable courtesans of Paris.

Marie-Amélia Laurent was staying in London for a while with her lover, a distinguished diplomat. He had taken a house in Mayfair, giving his mistress *carte blanche* to furnish it to her own taste, whilst he stayed ostensibly at a respectable hotel nearby.

Marie-Amélia was tall, dark and voluptuous, with black eyes, a slow, feline smile, and a most excellent command of the English language. She had taken her lover at his word and had transformed the house in which she proposed to stay for the next six months. The salon itself was a vision. It had a carpet like driven snow and drapes of white satin trimmed with scrolls of gold thread. The chandeliers looked like hanging diamonds, the red velvet sofas and chairs like opulent thrones from an Eastern palace.

Marie-Amélia gave a sudden laugh at the wonderment she saw in her visitor.

"You like it, eh? That is good, but it is nothing compared to my house in Paris. Ah, *chérie*, you should see that. It is the envy of everyone."

"I would love to see it, but I doubt that I shall ever go to Paris."

"Why not?" Marie-Amélia's brows rose. "It is the only civilised place on earth. You must come. With your looks, you could go far. I know a dozen men who would be delighted to have you for their mistress. They would wear you like their English cousins wear their medals."

Candace looked startled, and the Frenchwoman gave an earthy grin.

"Oh yes, they would not be ashamed of you and tuck you away in some obscure nest of love in the suburbs. In Paris it is different. Men are glad to be seen with a beautiful woman."

"Is it true that Frenchmen are wonderful lovers? I have heard it said that they are very passionate."

"No more so than the English, but they make more noise about it. I lived with an Englishman for four years; that is why I speak your tongue so well. Henry; ah, now he was a lover. Sometimes cruel in bed, but always a man. Paris is a city of uniforms these days, but the men who wear them are not heroes. You ask Cora Pearl."

"Cora Pearl?" Candace was impressed. Cora was one of the most famous courtesans of her day, her name as well-known in London as in Paris where she held court. "You know her?"

"Of course." Marie-Amélia was amused. "We are good friends. She is a bitch, of course, but we get along. She hates men, you know. Despises them when they cringe before her and beg her to whip them. She tells me all about it afterwards, and we laugh together. I don't like men either."

"Why does Cora Pearl hate men?"

Marie-Amélia shrugged. "For the same reason that I do, I suppose. They fawn and cringe and let us walk on them as if they were door-mats. How can you have affection for a door-mat? Have you a lover?"

"Well . . . yes."

Marie-Amélia put her head on one side.

"You do not sound sure, *ma petite*. Does that mean you do not know whether he loves you?"

Candace flushed. "Yes, I suppose so. I think he does, but he has never said so."

"He is good in bed, eh?"

"Very."

"Do you beat him?"

Candace looked startled for a moment; then she laughed, throwing back her head in genuine mirth. Marie-Amélia looked at Candace's slender white throat and the firm, perfect jawline, and nodded.

"Ah, then he is a man, yes?"

"Yes, he is."

"Does he treat you well? Give you jewels and clothes?"

"Yes."

"And a place like this?"

"No, I have my own home."

Her hostess clicked her tongue disapprovingly.

"That is not good. You should sell it and invest the money wisely. Then make him buy you another. Albert bought me this house. Come, let us go upstairs and you can see what this Englishman of yours should provide for you."

Candace followed obediently, dumb with admiration at the great winding stair covered in pale rose carpet, the handrail dressed in matching velvet, and the shimmering lights overhead. In the bedroom, Marie-Amélia had chosen pale yellow satin for the curtains and bed-hangings and a deep pile carpet of lightest green with a white skin rug by the hearth. When Candace had examined the delicate furniture and exquisite ornaments, they moved into the bathroom and she gasped aloud.

The bath was a vast shell of rose-coloured marble with gold taps fashioned like dolphins. The floor was marble of a lighter shade, with expensive bearskin rugs dotted here and there. There was a subtle smell of perfume from bottles of lotion and scent.

"It is . . . breathtaking." Candace was honest in her praise. "I have never seen anything like it before."

"It is nothing, as I have said. At home, in Paris, I have a better place than this, full of jade and onyx and precious pieces of gold and silver, with painted ceilings and tapestries on the wall." She closed the door of the bathroom. "Come, we will eat, and you shall talk to me about your English lover. Perhaps I can help you to tame him, eh? Every man can be brought to heel if you give the right commands. That is why they are all so dull."

"Blaise isn't dull."

"Blaise? That is an odd name."

"Is it? I hadn't thought about it."

"You blush when you speak of him. You are very much in love, aren't you? That is a pity; it is not a good start. One should never fall in love. Love gets in the way of success. Before you can rule a man's heart, you have to learn to rule your own, otherwise you can be hurt."

She led the way downstairs, and soon they were seated at the long oval table piled high with dishes of out-of-season fruit, caviare, cool wines.

The footman came in silently to serve the soup, and Candace stole a look round the dining-room, dazed by the costly rosewood furniture, the Sèvres china, and the stained glass in the windows.

Marie-Amélia took a noisy gulp of soup, for she had a hearty appetite and no time to bother with the niceties of table-manners when she was hungry.

"Now, what about this Englishman? Let us see if we can bring him to his senses, and if that doesn't work, be done with him and come back to France with me. With a body like yours, you could be the toast of Paris, wear clothes by Worth and Laferrière, and jewels from Cartiers. I know men who would be glad to buy you an hôtel like mine, and fill it with treasures from attic to cellar."

Candace smiled cautiously. She liked Marie-Amélia, but she was beginning to wonder whether, in return, Marie-Amélia, did not like her a little too much. She made her position clear at once, in case there should be any misunderstanding.

"I would rather have Blaise. He is all I want."

Marie-Amélia gave a faint, regretful shrug.

"So be it. Well, then, tell me about him, and I will shew you how to win his heart and control his pocket at the same time. It will not be difficult. Men are easy enough to handle if you know how."

She took a generous portion of peacock in galantine from the impassive servant and waited for Candace to begin her tale.

On the way home, Candace felt as if she had drunk too much. In fact, the intoxication was not caused by brandy or wine but by the bewilderment of the evening. She could understand why Marie-Amélia had become one of the great names of the Parisian *demi monde*. She had an animal-like quality; compelling, urgent, hard to resist. She had listened to all that Candace had told her, and had given her much advice.

Candace doubted whether anything that Marie-Amélia had said would help her to win Blaise, but she was glad she had met her and had seen her Mayfair dwelling. It would be something to aim for, if she did not succeed with Blaise.

Candace always kept a lofty target before her, for she never forgot her humble origins. She made herself remember them at least once a day, in case she should grow slack and lazy. She knew how painfully easy it was to slip back into squalor and poverty. To make sure that she did not fall into a similar trap, Candace made a practice of visiting the East End now and then, watching the raddled, grey-faced prostitutes begging men to take them for a few coppers. The streets were the only place for them; their sagging bodies their only currency.

She took her cloak off and gave it to Bessie Poke.

"I have a visitor in half an hour," she said as she mounted the stairs. "Shew him in when he comes. Don't wait up. I'll see him out myself."

The bedroom seemed very plain and modest after Marie-Amélia's. Like a schoolgirl's; clean and wholesome and dull. Perhaps she should change the drapes to-morrow; buy some made of satin of brighter hue. Then she gave a small laugh. It wouldn't make any difference. It wouldn't make it look like Marie-Amélia's boudoir.

She heard the tap on the door and rose to greet her guest, her smile intimate and welcoming as the man came into the room.

"Good-evening, Mr. Brown." She was always very polite to those who called on her. It was part of the service she gave them. "How are you to-night?"

"Very well, my dear."

Arthur Grey came forward, his hands outstretched, planting a firm kiss on her cheek.

"Yes, very well indeed, I think; all things considered."

FOUR

At eight o'clock on a foggy morning in mid-November, Blaise, Lord Westerbrook, returned to his home in Eaton Square.

His valet, Augustine Dean, welcomed him without surprise for he was well-used to his master and his ways, having known him since childhood. He helped Blaise to remove the elegant evening suit, brushing a microscopic speck of dust from the narrow rolled collar, laying the garments aside for pressing.

"A good night, my lord?"

Dean led the way into the bathroom, where piping hot water had been pumped up from the kitchen boiler, and a roaring fire burned in the grate. Dean was proud of the bathroom, for it was both luxurious and functional, with its pearl-grey carpet, mirrors, and marble-topped cabinets which housed all the necessities of a gentleman's toilet.

"Satisfactory. I won some money, and a woman whom I did not want. I gave her to Freddie Markington. He never seems to be able to get one for himself."

Dean smiled politely. He had long ago ceased to be shocked at the goings-on of the rich young set with whom his master associated.

He looked at Westerbrook again and his smile grew warmer. Really, Master Blaise had grown into a quite splendid creature. He let his eyes wander from the dark crisp hair to the cool blue eyes, and then to the arrogance of the high-bridged nose and firm, well-cut mouth. Blaise's body was in magnificent trim, despite the life of debauchery Dean was certain he lived. Broad-shouldered, slim-waisted, lean-flanked, with long, straight legs, and thin, strong hands which were at their best when he was on the back of a hunter.

Blaise finished his bath leisurely and put on the brocaded robe which had been warming by the fire.

Dean handed him some scented lotion to pat on the skin, and said tentatively:

"You have not thought, my lord, that perhaps you should grow a beard? Even a moustache with side-burns is considered very becoming."

"I have considered it and rejected it, as well you know." Blaise grinned amiably. "If God had wanted men to cover their faces with hair, He would not have given them the wit to invent the razor. I'm content as I am. Now what about breakfast?"

Westerbrook went down to the dining-room, nodding to the frilly-capped maids he encountered in the corridor. The house in Eaton Square was a large one and needed a big staff.

The dining-room was gracious and well-appointed, with grey-blue walls hung with sporting prints. On the sideboard, with its curved front and endless drawers housing cutlery, wine coasters and table linen, were covered silver dishes containing fish, rump-steaks, kidneys, bacon, eggs, ham and muffins.

Westerbrook helped himself to kidneys, bacon and toast, leaving the butler to pour coffee with a touch of hot milk.

Whilst he was drinking his second cup of coffee, he began to think about Candace Martin, and the faintest frown touched his brow. He would have to see her that night; he had failed to keep their last appointment and that would have angered her. Perhaps some small gift might soften her wrath. Then he grimaced. Why did he try to fool himself? Candace was not interested in his gifts, but in him.

He was not sure when he had first become aware that she regarded him in a different light from the rest of those who visited her in St. John's Wood, and that she was looking for something in him which wasn't there. It was awkward; damned awkward. He was still very fond of her and enjoyed sleeping with her, but he had no more to offer her than that.

For all his wild ways and apparent lack of care for the serious things of life, Blaise Westerbrook had a strong sense of responsibility to his family and its reputation. A discreet affair with a high-class courtesan would cause no ripple of disquiet amongst his august relations; marriage with a whore would split their world apart.

He was inclined to blame Candace; she was stepping outside the rules of the game. Not that she had intimated by so much as a word what was in her mind, but he had known right enough, and now he had to find some painless way of putting an end to their association. He cursed under his breath and went upstairs to dress.

At eleven o'clock, Sara Lessingham and Jenny arrived in Eaton Square. They were both very nervous, unhappy at the lie they had had to tell Aunt Rachel in order to venture upon their journey. It was made worse by the fact that Rachel accepted without question the proposed visit to an art gallery, and Sara felt ashamed and uneasy as she touched the bell and waited for Lord Westerbrook's door to open.

"I really do not know why I have come, Jenny," she said in a whisper. "After all, what can I tell him? And he will be old, like grandfather would have been, had he lived. How can I make him understand how worried I am?"

Jenny nodded in silent sympathy.

She had no time then to offer any consolation, for the door was opening and a liveried butler was gazing down at Sara in aloof enquiry.

When she ventured her request to see Lord Westerbrook, the man looked dubious, warning her with his stare that her demand was unlikely to meet with success. But after a moment, when he had assessed her quality, he stood back and allowed them to enter, shewing them into a morning-room furnished with quiet elegance.

When the door opened again Sara turned, expecting to find the butler shaking his head, ready to usher them out again, but instead she found herself facing a tall young man in a dark morning coat and fashionably tight trousers, who was regarding her with slight surprise from under raised eyebrows.

"Miss Lessingham? You wanted to see me?"

Sara could feel the blood leaving her cheeks, but she did not lose her poise as she shook her head.

"No, no. I am sorry, I think there has been some mistake. It was Lord Westerbrook whom I wished to see."

"I am Westerbrook."

Blaise crossed the room and took a closer look at his visitor. He could see that her surprise was as great as his, but beyond the consternation he could see the shadow of fear in the wide hazel eyes, and the trace of unhappiness in the line of the exquisite mouth.

He was used to looking at beautiful women and had thought himself immune from them, but there was something about this girl which almost made him catch his breath. It was not just her serene loveliness, or the flawless quality of her skin; not simply the grace with which she held herself, or the unbelievable line of her throat and jaw. It was something more subtle than that, too elusive to define at once; unsettling and unwelcome.

"You? But that is impossible."

"Oh?" He was cooler than he had meant to be, for he did not like to be disturbed emotionally before noon. He was not used to it, and it made him rather angry. "I can assure you that it is entirely possible. Why should it not be so?"

Sara blushed, aware of his irritation, and he found himself instantly bemused by the colour which flooded her cheeks.

"I . . . I . . . am sorry. You will think me not only rude, but slightly mad." She tried to make a joke of it and failed. "Indeed, that is really why I came. In case I am mad, you see."

"No, I don't." He was blunt. "Sit down, Miss Lessingham, and let us start again." He gestured her towards the sofa by the fire. "Tell me first why you were so astounded to find me in my own house."

"I . . . I . . . it is so difficult to explain. You will think me a fool."

"I doubt that. I do not make judgments so quickly. Why were you so surprised?"

"Because of grandfather's letter."

"Ah yes." Blaise gave a sudden smile which took the coldness from his eyes and lit his face with amusement. "I am sure that ought to tell me everything I want to know, but. . . ."

Sara gave a small laugh.

"I told you it was difficult to explain."

"Try. There is no hurry."

"I found a letter, or rather part of one, from my grandfather. It was written nine years ago, just before he died. He said that if ever I should need help, and if he were not there to give it to me, I should seek the aid of his friend, Lord Westerbrook. I assumed, of course, that Lord Westerbrook was older."

Blaise nodded slowly. "Yes, I see. What was your grandfather's name?"

"Jason Darby Lorrimer."

"Yes, I remember him. He was a close friend of my father's. My father died six years ago."

"Oh, I see."

He saw the light of hope die in her eyes and said quickly: "But your grandfather did tell you to come, and you were right to do so. As my father is no longer here, tell me."

"You?"

"Why not? I am at least as intelligent as my father was. Not yet so wise, perhaps, but how shall I become so unless I am given the chance to learn. Why do you need help?"

She still hesitated.

"I am not sure; that is the problem. I am not certain whether what has happened is real, or whether I have imagined it."

Blaise glanced at Jenny, who had withdrawn discreetly to

the far end of the room.

"Well, a fresh mind on the problem might help. What are you not sure is real or imagination?"

It was difficult to begin but once she had started, Sara found herself spilling out the whole story, hesitating now and then when the most frightening aspects had to be uncovered, trying to keep her voice steady and rational so that he would not think her hysterical.

He listened silently until she had finished, and then began to ask questions, not satisfied until he had every scrap of information he needed to complete the picture. Sara found that in the end she had told him not only about the fire and the nightmares; not simply of Uncle Arthur, Aunt Rachel and the family, but about Matthew Compton, Mrs. Bosey, Oliver's death, the matches, the incident in Regent Street, and even the creaking stairs.

She sat back, waiting for him to dismiss her fears as rubbish and rising to ring for the butler to shew her firmly to the door. She watched him as he gazed into the fire, one part of her mind divorced from her troubles as she admired the breadth of his shoulders and the clean, firm lines of his face.

Finally he smiled at her.

"I need time to think," he said and rose to his feet. "I told you I did not make judgments quickly."

"Of course not." She got up hastily. "I understand. I should not have come."

"Of course you should; it was your grandfather's wish. Give me time; I will consider what you have told me."

He took her hand for a moment and felt it tremble in his.

When she and Jenny had gone, he went back to his bedroom where Augustine Dean was tidying a drawer. Dean had many more uses than as a mere valet, and it was Blaise's habit to talk freely to him about most subjects, for Augustine's discretion and tight-lipped secrecy was well-known to him.

He outlined what Sara Lessingham had told him, keeping the facts free from emotion.

"And that is her story," he said finally. "I do not know whether she is a trifle unbalanced, or whether someone is trying to make her appear so."

"There would have to be a reason. If it is someone else, there must be a motive. Is she rich?"

"Apparently not. Her father left just enough for her upbringing, and her grandfather had nothing left to bequeath her save some trifle which she will get when she is eighteen."

"She is very young. I am surprised that her aunt let her come here."

"She doesn't know that she did. She thought the girl was going to an art gallery." Blaise threw himself down on the bed and looked up at the moulded ceiling. "You're right, of course. If it is someone else, there has to be a reason. Since it is not the obvious one, money, it must be something else, but what?"

"Is she beautiful, my lord?"

"Very," Westerbrook said without expression, but Augustine turned his head slightly to regard his master with interest.

"Could that be it? Jealousy?"

"I cannot see how, or who would be sufficiently jealous of her to make them take such steps as these."

"You said, my lord, that her cousin died recently."

"Yes, he fell down the area stairs in a fog and broke his neck."

"An accident?"

"Oh yes, it would seem so. There was no question of anything else."

"Then I confess myself baffled."

"And I, at any rate for the moment."

There was another silence, then Blaise said slowly:

"Of course, we cannot dismiss entirely the other possibility."

"That there is no one else?"

"Yes, that most of what has happened is in her imagination. There is the history of her childhood; the fire and her parents' death."

"You think she could be . . . well . . . not quite normal?"

"It is not impossible, but I am not yet ready to condemn her as such." He sat up and clasped his hands round his knees. "I think we will try to find out more about Miss Lessingham and her family. We have heard her version of them and the house in Candle Square, which she doesn't like. Now we will do some investigations of our own."

"But how?"

"We will have them watched. It must be done with discretion, of course. That man we used when Fox-Bannister was being blackmailed . . . what was his name?"

"Roper. Arnold Roper."

"Get hold of him. Tell him I want to see him."

"Yes, my lord."

"I may even pay a visit to Candle Square myself. The son of an old friend of Jason Lorrimer, paying a duty call to see Lorrimer's granddaughter. What could be more innocent than that? I would like to see some of these people for myself."

Candace Martin looked at the small jewelled clock on the mantelpiece and frowned. It was growing late, and she had been waiting for Blaise Westerbrook to arrive for the last hour.

She had been unhappy since noon, when one of Blaise's kitchen maids, whom she paid to keep her supplied with information about him, called to say that her master had had a visitor that morning. An unexpected caller, very lovely, so Rook, the butler, had said. The thought lay like a rasp on Candace's mind, scratching at her self-confidence, nurturing the seed of jealousy which she tried so hard to hide from Blaise.

The maid had no idea who the girl was. The butler had refused to add a name when pressed by Blaise's cook to divulge more information. All the maid had known was that the caller was beautiful, and had stayed with his lordship for nearly an hour.

Candace got up and walked over to the fireplace, staring at herself in the mirrored overmantel. Was it her own fault that Blaise was not as interested in her as he should be? Had she failed somehow to please him? If Blaise's visitor was beautiful, so was she.

She knew she had not failed him in bed. It was many years since she had first tried to please a man. Now, she knew exactly how to do it, for she had made it her business to learn her trade well, and Blaise had seemed satisfied enough.

Was he ashamed of her? Certainly he had never invited her to his home, but she had not expected that, yet he had seemed pleased enough to be seen with her at Mott's and the Argyll, or to acknowledge her when she donned her trim, well-cut riding habit and shewed off her paces in Hyde Park.

If she was going to be able to coax him into marriage, or even into a more permanent liaison of a different nature, she would have to work harder. She must try again, concealing her doubts and rancour, making him laugh and relax before the time came for them to leave the empty wine-glasses and to go into the bedroom together.

When Bessie Poke shewed Westerbrook into the room, Candace turned and smiled at him, slowly and lovingly, one hand outstretched.

"Blaise. Dearest Blaise."

"I am late; forgive me."

"It is not important. You are here."

"I have been busy."

The green eyes were hidden for a moment under the darkened lashes. He had not always been too busy to arrive on time. In spite of herself, she could hear the sharpening note in her own voice.

"Yes, I am sure you have."

He saw the anger in her, despite her efforts to conceal it, feeling a slight stab of surprise, but he said nothing as he handed her the small package he had taken from his pocket.

"A gift? How nice."

His eyes narrowed as she opened the jewel-box and took out the bracelet of diamonds and pearls. Candace was on edge to-night; put out, perhaps, because he had been late, or because he had not been to see her for a few days. He said lightly:

"A beautiful bauble for a beautiful woman."

"Do men make gifts of baubles to women, or only to prostitutes?"

He sat back and watched the light play on the gems.

"To both, I imagine. Why do you ask?"

"Because I wanted to know. Do you really think of me as a woman?"

"I should have thought the answer to that was obvious," he returned dryly. "We have known one another long enough for you to draw your own conclusions.

"I suppose so. Will you have some wine?"

"I think we had both better have some wine. A good vintage is remarkably relaxing."

She bit her lip. It was a reprimand, and she knew it. She got up to pour the wine, forcing herself to be calm.

"What have you been doing to-day?" she asked politely, as if the answer was of no particular importance.

"Nothing of consequence. I paid a few duty calls; had lunch at Fowley's; went to a concert."

"And entertained an attractive young woman at Eaton Square."

The words were out of her mouth before she could stop them, and she felt her cheeks crimson with embarrassment. She had not meant to speak of the matter, but somehow her normal self-control had failed her, and he was raising his eyebrows in distant surprise.

She was forced into a quick explanation.

"A mutual friend of ours saw her." She hoped the lie was not too obvious. In a way, of course, it wasn't a lie at all. She and Blaise both knew his maid. "It is not my business, I know. I shouldn't have mentioned it."

He drank his wine slowly, waiting until the spurt of irritation inside himself had died down before speaking. He was right; Candace was on edge. Otherwise she would never have given herself away. He'd been right about the other matter too.

She was taking a good deal more interest in him than was normal in such an arrangement as theirs.

"Oh, that girl." He was very casual. "Her grandfather was a friend of my father's. She thought my father was still alive and it was he whom she came to see. A mistake, no more than that. She didn't stay long."

Candace wanted to shout at him that she knew exactly how long the girl had stayed, but that would have driven him straight out of the house. Instead, she nodded and smiled brightly.

"Of course, but as I have said, it is no business of mine. It is just that I like to hear what you do, Blaise, and how you spend your days. It makes me feel closer to you."

"You would do better to consider how I spend my nights, or at least some of them." He was teasing her now, laying down his glass as he got up and held out his hand. "Your gown is beautiful, but would you be offended if I removed it?"

She giggled, suddenly very happy again as they walked upstairs together.

She let him undress her, scolding him lovingly when he threw aside the dress as if it were a rag, but then there was no more time for words as he kissed her on the mouth and pulled her over to the bed.

Later, when she lay in his arms, the worry came back once more. She knew she should not mention the matter again, but the small devil inside her was pricking her with red-hot forks.

"That girl."

"Mm?"

He was half-asleep, content to feel the warmth of Candace's body close to his. If he had been really honest with himself, he would have had to admit that his love-making that night had been a trifle mechanical and that he was actually thinking about Sara Lessingham and her lost, unhappy eyes. He stirred, forcing himself to pay attention.

"Blaise, that girl."

"What girl?"

"The girl you saw to-day. Will you see her again?"

It was too late to quarrel. He was tired and wanted to sleep, so he avoided the issue.

"I doubt it. Why should I? Stop talking, woman. Have you nothing better to do?"

She could feel the moisture under her closed lids as she turned to him again. In spite of his arms about her and the feel of his lips against her breast, she knew he was lying; she could hear it in his voice. Whatever Blaise said in words, he was planning to see the girl again.

Whilst Arthur Grey continued to press Sara to consider marriage with Sidney, and Sidney himself showered her with small, shy attentions, Matthew Compton was also laying siege to her heart.

In spite of the black disapproval of Grey and his wife, Matthew had continued to pay frequent calls, mostly on the grounds that he wished to see how his aunt was, but, in fact, solely to seize whatever chance was available to talk to Sara.

On a dreary Saturday morning he called to take coffee with Mercy Thorne, delighted to find Sara with her in the morning-room. Mercy had a bad cold, making her deafer than usual, and she had withdrawn to the window where she could see to sew.

"I am glad to see you again." Matthew's pleasure was obvious. "It seems a long time since we were alone."

Sara felt herself stiffen as if to prepare to withstand some assault, chiding herself instantly for her folly. Matthew meant no harm. He was simply being kind and offering his friendship. She must not hurt him by rejecting it too obviously.

"We are never alone." She made a small joke of it. "We aren't alone now. Mercy is here."

"It is the nearest to being alone which is possible. Aunt Mercy grows deafer, have you noticed?"

"Yes, it is sad for her."

"I may not have another chance to speak to you like this,

and there is something I must say, Sara."

The look in his eyes had changed and his voice was serious. "Oh?"

"Sara, you must know how I feel about you."

"Matthew! You mustn't...."

"Yes, I must. Why do you think I keep coming here?"

"To see Mercy."

"You know that is not so. I would meet her elsewhere if that were the reason, seeing how unwelcome my presence is. But if I were to do that, I should never see you."

"Matthew, you must not...."

"I want to marry you."

"It is impossible! I don't want to talk about it."

"You must! You cannot shut your ears to what I am saying. Sara, don't you feel anything for me?"

"I ... I...."

"Yes, I know, I know. That is an unfair question." He leaned forward to touch her hand. "I don't expect you to answer it now. I know that I should be speaking to your uncle, but he is not friendly. I must wait for the right moment."

"But, Matthew, I...."

She was desperate, looking hopelessly towards the window where Mercy sat oblivious to her distress. She was searching feverishly for the right words, when he rose and said quickly:

"I must go now; I have another appointment. But I will come again soon. Wait while I say good-bye to Aunt Mercy."

When he had kissed his aunt and bade her not to trouble herself to move, Sara walked from the morning-room into the hall with Matthew by her side. It was a gloomy morning and everything seemed shadowed and shuttered, the heavy velvet drapes hanging like a pall in the archway which led to the drawing-room.

"There is something else I must tell you when next I come." He kept his voice low but clear. "I think that you may be in danger in this house, Sara. I have felt it for some time. If you marry me, I can take you away from here."

"Danger?" Her head turned quickly. "What kind of danger? Why do you say that?"

"I can't explain now, there isn't time. I will tell you when I come again. Take care, Sara, and think about what I have said. I would be good to you, you know."

Sara said nothing, waiting until Aggie Lowther came to shew Matthew out, staring after him and not turning back to the morning-room in time to see the velvet drapes move slightly and then fall slowly back into their normal folds.

Compton was as good as his word, and on the following day he presented himself in time for tea.

Rachel's lips thinned as he was shewn in, and she cast Mercy Thorne a black look. Really, something would have to be done about this young man. He was becoming a positive nuisance and if she were not mistaken Rebecca was harbouring thoughts about him which she had no business to do. Rachel had noticed that hitherto most of Compton's visits had been timed to coincide with Arthur's absence from the house, but to-day Matthew had not bothered to avoid him, walking into the sitting-room as bold as you please, as if he were one of the family.

"Please forgive the intrusion." Compton bowed to Aunt Rachel with charming deference. "I came to see how Aunt Mercy was. She had such a bad cold that I was concerned for her."

"No need to be," returned Rachel tightly. "As you see, she is well enough to attend to her duties."

"Yes, and I am glad, but then Mercy never gives in easily, does she?" He turned to Arthur. "I hope you are well, sir."

Arthur chewed his bottom lip. He shared Rachel's distaste for the young man, but if he had to be got rid of it must be done carefully. He could not order him out of the house as if he were a tradesman. Somewhere along the line their blood mingled. It was a difficult situation, but no problem was without solution.

"Yes, yes, I'm fit enough."

Since there was obviously no question of Matthew leaving, Rachel was forced to invite him to take tea, the suggestion wrung from her as Aggie and Jenny arrived with the trays.

Sara was glad that Matthew paid her no special attention. She felt herself blushing as he took his seat next to her, praying that no one would notice her unwonted colour.

"It is good to see you again, Matthew." Rebecca was smiling at him intimately, trying to convey the impression to all present that she was the real reason for his visit. "Are you still busy in your solicitor's office?"

"Very." He returned her smile, but formally, as if they had only just met. "The work is very interesting."

"Will you soon be a solicitor yourself?"

"Quite soon, I hope." He turned away to look at Sara. "And you, Miss Lessingham, are you well?"

Sara murmured something, glad of the diversion when Henrietta began to pour the tea.

"Father, will you take this please?"

Grey nodded, handing the first cup to Rachel, coming back for the next.

"Pass this to Sara, father, will you? It is for Mr. Compton. This is yours, Sidney. This is Sara's and yours, father."

There was a momentary bustle as cups went from hand to hand, Aggie filling up the teapot from the spirit kettle, Jenny charged with taking round the plates of thin cucumber sandwiches.

Conversation became general, and for a while it seemed that the others had forgotten their dislike of Matthew Compton as they talked of music, painting, and the latest news of the Court.

It was five o'clock when Compton dropped his teacup. The clock on the mantelpiece had just struck the hour, and they turned to look at him, frowning at his clumsiness until they realised that he was doubled up as if in great pain, slumping in his chair as he began to groan.

"Matthew! What is it, what is it?"

Mercy Thorne got stiffly from her seat and hurried to her nephew's side, the others rising too and staring down at the afflicted man.

"Good heavens, what is wrong?" Rachel was sharp, for she had been genuinely startled by the sounds her unwanted guest was making. "Henrietta, what is wrong with the man? Is he drunk?"

"Of course not, mama." Henrietta's face was pale. "He is ill. Aggie, go and get Dr. Blackmore, and hurry!"

Aggie ran from the room, whilst Grey and Sidney pulled the ailing Matthew back into the chair.

"What is it? Are you in pain?"

Compton grimaced, the sweat standing out in beads on his forehead.

"Yes . . . yes . . . terrible pain. Don't know what is wrong . . . just pain. . . ."

"Shall we get you some water?"

"Couldn't drink . . . couldn't drink it . . . the pain. . . . ."

They stood by helplessly as he doubled up again, Rachel closing her eyes in disgust as he started to retch. They could not move him, nor could they give him aid, and they exchanged worried glances until the doctor arrived and drove them all from the room.

Later, when Matthew had recovered slightly and had been sent home in a cab, the doctor came to the drawing-room to announce the fact.

"He'll do. Been very sick; best thing for him. Got rid of it."

"Rid of what?" Grey was terse. "Rid of what, Dr. Blackmore? What was wrong with him?"

"Eaten something." Blackmore had washed his hands but he was still rubbing them together as if to ensure they were perfectly clean and dry. "Something he ate."

"Poison?"

They all turned to stare at Rebecca, and Arthur Grey said quickly:

"Be quiet, Rebecca! That is an absurd suggestion. How could he have been poisoned?"

"Yes, probably it was poison of some kind," the doctor went on. "Had all the symptoms, you know."

"But that is impossible." Grey tugged at his moustache in consternation. "He'd been here an hour or more. Surely if it had been something he ate for luncheon, it would have shewn before now."

"Oh yes, it wasn't his luncheon. Something he'd taken later than that. Well, I must be off. Other calls to make. Good-day, Mr. Grey."

Henrietta rang for Aggie, and when Dr. Blackmore was safely off the premises they turned to each other in anxiety.

"He did seem ill." Sidney shook his head. "Will he be all right on his own, do you think?"

"Is there anyone to care for him at his lodgings, Mercy?"

"What dear?"

"Anyone at his lodgings to look after him?" Henrietta repeated the question with commendable patience. "Sidney wondered if he would be all right on his own."

"Oh yes, there's Mrs. Samuels. She's his landlady. I wish I could go with him though. Poor boy, he was so ill."

"I don't think mama would want you to do that." Henrietta was firm. "If there's someone there, that will be good enough. Dr. Blackmore says he's over the worst."

"What happened, do you think?" Rebecca's eyes sparkled with something which made Sara's nerves jump. "Do you think he ate some berries on the way here?"

"Of course he didn't, Rebecca, don't be so foolish."

Rebecca tossed her head, her colour a little higher.

"Is it so foolish, Henrietta? Then if he didn't do that, what did he eat which made him ill?"

"I really do not know, but...."

"One of our sandwiches, do you think?"

They stared at her, angry with her for making such a suggestion.

"But I ate three of those." Sidney's face grew a shade whiter. "Father, do you think that I too will...."

"Certainly not." Grey was brusque. "Rebecca, I forbid you to...."

"But, father, if it wasn't something he had here, what was it?"

"I don't know, but it couldn't have been the sandwiches or the cakes. We all ate them too."

"The tea then?"

"We all drank that."

"From our own cups."

Grey took a deep breath. "What do you mean, Rebecca, from our own cups? Of course we drunk from our own cups. How else could we drink our tea?"

"There was nothing wrong with the teapot, papa." Rebecca was smiling secretively in spite of Grey's growing anger. "You have all admitted it, for how else would we have escaped? It must have been in the cup which Matthew had."

"The cups were perfectly clean, I can assure you." Mercy bridled instantly at the suggestion that her housekeeping was at fault.

"I'm sure it was, Mercy, but something could have been put into Matthew's cup, couldn't it?"

There was a stricken silence, the point which Rebecca was making too obvious now to be ignored.

"I saw Henrietta pour Matthew's tea." Rebecca's face was smug and self-contained as if she were hugging herself inside. "Then, of course, the cup was passed to him. You had it last, didn't you, Sara? You held it for him for a moment or two whilst he put his plate down."

Sara felt everybody's eyes turn on her, examining her anew in the light of Rebecca's statement. She tried to speak, but her mouth seemed to be filled with dust.

"That will do, Rebecca." Grey meant it this time. "I have

heard quite enough of this nonsense. Whatever that unfortunate young man had to eat or drink which made him ill, he did not get it in this house. Now I will not have another word said on this matter, is that clear?"

He waited until they all nodded their obedience, then he made for the door, turning to look back at them for a second.

"Remember. Not another word is to be said. It was an accident, and that is the end of it."

FIVE

On a foggy mid-November day, Sara Lessingham received the first of the anonymous letters. It came with a number of others.

She took the letters to her room, in no hurry to open them, moving the muslin curtains to watch the dense saffron blanket roll nearer to the house. She could hear people about but she could not see them. Then she turned from the window and considered the envelope in her hand. Thick white paper with bold black letters which looked important.

When she finally opened it and began to read, she felt the shock hit her with such a force that it took her breath away. She tried to stop reading, but she couldn't. The words had an hypnotic effect, holding her rigid, refusing her the easy way out. She only understood part of what it said; many of the words she had never heard of before, but she knew they were dirty and evil. The unknown writer accused her of sexual malpractices with Oliver and with Uncle Arthur, explicit in detail, terrifying in malice.

Sara sat on the end of the bed, her legs no longer able to bear her weight.

Whoever had written it had meant to injure her as surely as if they had beaten her with a stick, only this was worse than any stick. Worse, even, than her fall in Regent Street. So it was not her imagination; that hadn't been an accident at all. There was someone trying to hurt her. Whoever it was knew all about her, and Oliver and Uncle Arthur too. There were small references which shewed the knowledge to be intimate, and suddenly Sara felt sick.

She could not avoid the obvious any longer. Someone in the house must have written the letter; who else would know so much about her. But who, in the family, hated her that much, and who would write in terms which she, Sara, hardly understood?

Sara took a deep breath and stood up. She must destroy the letter, so that no one else could ever see it. In a moment she would make an excuse to go to the kitchen and, whilst no one was looking, would burn it.

She rubbed her cheeks to bring some colour back to them and then went downstairs to the morning-room, her head held high, the letter folded into a small wad in her pocket.

"An interesting development, Augustine."

Blaise Westerbrook was dressing for dinner. It was a matter of duty. Later he could go on to the Haymarket, or perhaps to Candace's.

"Yes, my lord. What else did Mr. Roper have to say?"

"Not much more. Simply that this nephew of Grey's housekeeper, Matthew Compton, called to take tea with the family and became violently ill."

"And no one else was affected?"

"No. Of course, Compton might well have eaten some bad food before he arrived at Candle Square, yet taken with other things it cannot be ignored."

"Other things?"

"Oliver Grey's death."

"But that was an accident."

"So we are told." Blaise's blue eyes were reflective and his mouth had grown hard. "Certainly there is no proof to the contrary, yet consider it in the light of the things which Sara Lessingham had to say. That business in Regent Street, for instance, and the matches which were found in her drawer. Alone, not one of them is of particular significance, but put them together, Augustine, and what do you have?"

"I am not sure."

"Neither am I, and that is why I went to see Arthur Grey this morning."

"Did he think that strange, my lord?"

"No, why should he? I simply told him that I had heard from an acquaintance that the granddaughter of my father's old friend lived in Candle Square, and I was merely paying my respects."

"Did you see Miss Lessingham?"

"No." Blaise's slight frown had gone. "No, I was told she was out, but fortunately Grey was there."

"What kind of man is he?"

"Rather what I expected. A business man; chemicals, I believe. Successful, I would judge. Kindly enough, and obviously fond of the girl. When I offered my condolences on the death of his son, his grief was genuine. As he spoke of him, he seemed to wilt somehow, and he could not bring himself to meet my eye."

"Did you see anyone else?"

"Yes, the housekeeper, but only briefly. A pale, colourless woman with something quite different below the surface, I suspect. Oh, and the parlour maid who brought in the coffee. A dolly-mop, if ever I saw one."

"It doesn't tell us very much, my lord, does it?"

"Not much, and it could still be a matter of coincidence on the one hand and Sara's imagination on the other."

"Shall I tell Arnold Roper his services are no longer required?"

Blaise stood up, smiling down at Augustine Dean in a way which made his valet twitch with brief alarm.

"Oh no, Augustine, not yet. We must have more patience than that. If the girl is a trifle mad, we shall know in the course of time. If she is not, then we are all that stands between her and whoever is doing these things. No, we shall not give up yet."

Two days later Sara went down to the kitchen to look for

Mercy Thorne. She had always liked the kitchen, even as a child, for it had seemed to her to be the most cheerful and friendly place in the house.

There was no sign of Mrs. Tamworth or Aggie, and for a moment Sara was content to stand and drink in the comfort which surrounded her. The fire was welcoming, the rocking chairs by the hearth a temptation to be lazy. On the high mantelshelf were inexpensive pieces of pottery and a stiff likeness of the Queen and her unsmiling consort. It was a lived-in place, where one could relax.

After a while Sara left the kitchen and went along the narrow passage to the larder. When she heard voices she stopped, not meaning to listen to things not intended for her ears, but caught by the sound of her own name.

"What is Miss Sara's legacy, Mrs. Tamworth?"

"No one knows. 'Ere, Aggie, 'and me that dish of apples, there's a good girl. Nothin' much, of course. I've 'eard mistress say that times enough. Just a piece of jewellery they think; nothin' of value."

"So she'll need a rich husband." Aggie giggled. "Do you think she's pretty?"

"Oh, she's 'andsome enough. Bit thin for my taste, and lookin' peaky nowaday. Seems a little nervy to me. All that fuss because she 'ad a fall, and what about them matches in 'er drawer? We might 'ave been burnt alive in our beds."

Aggie gave a shrill squeal, but she was more interested in gossiping than in the thought of sudden death.

"Miss Thorne's nephew's sweet on 'er; anyone can see that."

"Watch your tongue. It's not your place to say such things."

"Well, it's true enough." Aggie sulked. "You don't see 'em together like I do. He's got no eyes for anyone else when she's in the room. You should see Miss Rebecca's face. She don't like it at all, I can tell you. She fancies 'im 'erself."

"'Ow can you tell?" Mrs. Tamworth was tempted in spite of herself.

"Easy enough." Aggie was scornful, superior in her judgment of the human condition. "She's in love with 'im."

"Master won't like this young man paying attention to Miss Sara. 'E wants 'er to marry Sidney."

"I wouldn't marry 'im. 'E's a boy, with no go in 'im. I should know."

"Oh? How, pray, miss, do you know such a thing?"

Aggie's laughter was low and knowledgeable.

"Never you mind, Mrs. T; I know."

"You know too much for your own good, Aggie Lowther."

"Maybe. I told you that some lord came to see the master, didn't I?"

"You've told me a dozen times or more."

Aggie was silent for a moment, but then her mind went back to the family again. "Do you think Miss Sara will marry Sidney?"

"I've no idea, I'm sure. If she's funny in the 'ead, as some say, perhaps she'd better. Then she could stay 'ere so master could keep an eye on 'er."

"Jenny doesn't think she's mad."

"Jenny's too young to know about these things, and she's far too familiar with Miss Sara. They're always talkin' together. Master wouldn't like that either if 'e knew. Jenny's a servant, same as us. Miss Sara's family. Jenny should keep to her place. And, by the way, what was you doin' out of bed in the middle of the night, may I ask?"

"Middle of the night? You must 'ave been dreamin', like Miss Sara, Mrs. T. I didn't get up last night."

"You'll get yourself into trouble afore you're done, my girl, see if you don't. Don't you think everyone's as blind as the mistress."

"I don't know what you mean, I'm sure." Aggie was indignant, but there was the trace of a satisfied purr beneath the surface. "I stayed in me bed last night, like a decent Christian. I wouldn't walk about this 'ouse at night for anythin'."

"Oh that stuff and nonsense! I've never seen nothin'."

"Others 'ave, and I'd not take the chance. It's 'aunted,

everyone says so."

"I don't," said Mrs. Tamworth with crushing finality. "And now be off with you. We've a lot to do before lunch, and them potatoes need peelin'."

Sara ran back along the corridor before they could see her, hastening upstairs to the morning-room to find that Mercy was already there. When she was free to slip away, she went to her room to think about cook's talk with Aggie Lowther. She refused to dwell on their obvious opinion of her mental stability, glossing over their contempt for Sidney and his potential prowess as a husband. Instead, she thought about her grandfather, the mention of the small legacy reminding her again that she knew so little about him.

Suddenly it seemed important to know more of him, as if he were an anchor from her happier childhood. She wanted to ask someone questions about him; even to know what he had left her to remind her of him.

It was then that she caught sight of a note from Victoria Roseby, an old friend of her mother's. The note was on the dressing table waiting to be answered. Victoria might know. She must have known Jason Lorrimer, for she had been a close friend of his daughter's.

Victoria Roseby answered Sara's request by return of post.

"I knew your grandfather, of course," wrote Victoria. "A kind man and a very shrewd one. We were all very surprised when he made those bad investments, for it was not at all like him to make such a mistake. But, there, even the cleverest of us cannot always avoid errors. As to his Will, my dear, I know nothing about it. He did not have much to leave, of course, after things went wrong for him. I know that it was made when he was dying, for I met his doctor, whom I knew, and was bold enough to ask the question. The doctor witnessed it, but he has since gone to Africa. There were few people in the house at the time, or so I understand, and the maid had to be asked to witness it. She has since died, I believe, but perhaps the nurse who was also there may still be alive. Her name was Flora, and she used to live in Camberwell at number four Peak Road. I doubt if she will be able to tell you much, but as she nursed your grandfather in his last illness, you may find some comfort in getting in touch with her. I only wish I knew who his solicitor was."

Sara put the letter aside, not quite prepared to embark upon correspondence with the nurse yet, but reassured to know that there was still a link with her grandfather when she was ready.

It was time now to get ready to take tea with some of Aunt Rachel's friends, and Sara changed into her moss-green foulard with the velvet trim and began to search for the thin silk scarf which she normally wore with it. She frowned when she found that it was missing, for she was certain she had folded it carefully and put it away not two days before. She tried the other drawers of the chest and then the wardrobe, in case she had absent-mindedly hung it amongst the frocks and cloaks, but it was nowhere to be seen.

She shrugged, puzzled but not unduly worried. She would ask Jenny later. Perhaps she had found it and tucked it away somewhere. She smoothed her hair, and then turned to the window.

She didn't know why she had chosen to look out at that moment. It was a sudden impulse which made her move the curtains aside and look down into the street, and as she did so she saw an old woman by the kerb, looking up at the house. There were other people passing by, but somehow the woman caught Sara's attention immediately. Although it was a long way down, Sara had the feeling that she was looking straight up at her, hunched in a shabby old dress and thick shawl to keep out the cold.

She knew also, although afterwards she told herself it was mere fancy, that the old woman was hostile. There was something about the stillness of her pose and the fixed upward stare which could not be mistaken, and Sara's fingers trembled as she let the curtain fall back into place.

It was absurd, of course. She was imagining things again.

She didn't know the woman, and it was impossible that the woman could know her, never mind shew hostility to her.

As she walked downstairs, she found herself thinking about Blaise Westerbrook. It was not the first time that her thoughts had turned to him since their meeting, and she had felt ridiculously happy when she had learned that he had called to see Uncle Arthur, regretful that she had not seen him herself. Now, she would have liked to tell him about the old woman, so that he could have laughed her fears away, but, of course, even if he had been there, she would not really have dared to mention the matter.

He must already think her a strange sort of girl, full of stupid fancies and unfounded apprehensions, and she did not want to increase his doubts by adding new absurdities. But even if she had not mentioned the old woman, she would still have liked to talk to him. She wondered if he were interested in books and paintings, as she was, or whether he had no time for anything but the fast life which Uncle Arthur said he pursued. Uncle Arthur had mentioned Blaise's visit without particular expression in his voice, but when Sara ventured an innocent question, he had been guarded, his mouth pinched at the corners.

He was not really the kind of man to be encouraged to visit Candle Square, Grey had said somewhat censoriously. Not that Westerbrook was likely to call again, but nevertheless he was best forgotten. She, Sara, was too young to understand the reasons, Grey had gone on, but she would have to take his word that Westerbrook was unsuitable. There had been a vague hint of gambling and, even worse, of women, and then the subject had been closed.

Women. Sara was nearly at the door of the sitting-room when she felt something very like a spasm of pain. She wondered what kind of women Blaise Westerbrook knew, and how intimate he was with them. It was an impertinent thought and one to be instantly dismissed from her mind, but it was not so easy to be rid of it. She could see the contours of his face in her mind's eye, and the firm line of his jaw and chin. She had known at once he was not the same kind of man that she was used to; not like Uncle Arthur, Matthew, or Sidney.

Westerbrook was hard, like a diamond, underneath his easy charm. He lived in a world which was totally beyond her comprehension, indulging in pastimes which Uncle Arthur had glossed over quickly. She was a fool, even to think of Blaise, for once he had shewn her to the door he had probably dismissed her from his mind as if she had never existed.

And yet he had called to see Uncle Arthur; he had not entirely forgotten her. Sara's eyes brightened as she opened the door, smiling with something near to happiness as she crossed the floor to join the circle round Aunt Rachel's couch.

SIX

It was a Sunday early in December. Compton, now completely recovered from his illness, had contrived to get Sara to one end of the drawing-room, sufficiently far away from the family for conversation of a private nature to be possible.

"Dear Sara, of course you didn't have anything to do with what happened to me."

"But you said...."

"I said that I would tell everyone that this was so."

"Do they need to be told?"

She could hear the faint panic in her own voice, forcing herself to be calm in case Henrietta or Arthur Grey should turn their heads in her direction.

"No, no, I suppose not, but I did hear...."

"What?"

"That Rebecca said something which might have made people wonder."

Sara took a deep breath.

"Yes; yes she did, but I do not think anyone took any notice of her. Nothing more was said. Uncle Arthur does not want us to talk of it. He is sure that it was something you ate before you got here."

"Then I will confirm it. I will tell them that this is what happened, but, Sara, if I do this for you, will you in turn do something for me?"

"What? And you are doing me no service by telling the truth. You speak as if you are protecting me from something which I did, but I did nothing. You know that."

"Hush, Sara, hush! They will hear us. No, no, I know you

did nothing, but it will do no harm if I were to say that I now know the cause of my sudden illness, will it?"

"No, I suppose not."

She was reluctant to accede any point which might give him the impression that she was accepting favours from him.

"Well then, that is that. Now, have you thought any more about what I said before?"

She shot him a look, uneasy when she saw Aunt Rachel turn towards them.

"What did you say?"

"That I wanted to marry you. You can't have forgotten that. Did it mean so little to you that you have forgotten all about it?"

"It is not that. Matthew, we cannot talk of such things now. I told you then it was impossible."

"Nothing is impossible if one wants to achieve it badly enough."

Sara hesitated. She thought there was something in Matthew's voice she had not heard before, as if he were suppressing some strong emotion under conventional words. Before she could dwell on what that emotion might be, Matthew spoke again.

"Think about it; that is all I ask. Don't make a decision now, if you are not ready, but think about it."

"Matthew, I...."

"Sara."

Aunt Rachel's voice broke into her distress,

"Come here, you will take cold over there by the window. Come and sit next to me, and Henrietta will give you some more tea." She eyed Compton up and down as he crossed the room with Sara. "No doubt you wish to be going, Mr. Compton. We will not detain you. Mercy will see you out."

Compton managed a civil smile, but Sara could see something simmering under the mask. He was angry and hurt, and so was Mercy Thorne, who rose to obey Rachel, her cheeks flushed with unusual colour.

"Really, Arthur." Rachel glared at her husband as the door closed. "You must do something about that young man. Are we forever to have him under our feet? You must speak to Mercy. Tell her that he is not to come here again."

Arthur Grey looked up. Sara thought he seemed tired, and that there were new lines round his eyes and scoring crevices beside his mouth. It was natural enough; he was still grieving for Oliver. Perhaps if he could have brought himself to speak of his elder son it would have helped, but he seemed reluctant to make even a mention of his name.

"Yes, my dear." His voice was weary too, accepting the inevitable about an unwelcome task which could not be put off any longer. "Yes, I will see what I can do."

He laid his cup down, making his excuses as he left the drawing-room and crossed the hall to the study. At the door he paused. It would not be easy, but for once Rachel was right. Something would have to be done about Matthew Compton.

On the following Saturday the blow fell. The day had been much like any other until three o'clock in the afternoon when Rachel Grey found that her most valuable diamond ring was missing.

The news of the loss soon travelled round the house, and before long everyone was gathered in her room, listening to her shrill alarm.

"I had it only yesterday. Henrietta, you gave it to me, if you recall, when I was dressing for dinner."

"Yes, mama, that is so." Henrietta was flustered for once, for she had already had the task of searching her mother's jewel-case and dressing-table for the missing ring. "Yes, you wore it yesterday."

"What did you do with it when you took it off, my dear?" Grey did not sound worried yet, as if he expected the ring to turn up at any minute in some unlikely place where Rachel had put it in an absent-minded moment. "Can you remember?"

"Of course I can remember, Arthur. I put it in my jewel-case."

"Then it should still be there." Arthur refused to be ruffled by her tone. "Have you and Henrietta looked properly?"

"Of course we have. Do you suppose I should declare it lost until we had searched thoroughly? It is not there. See for yourself."

Grey frowned, turning the bracelets and necklaces over gently with one finger and finally shrugging his agreement.

"No, my dear, you're right. It isn't there."

"Of course it isn't. I told you that. But where is it?"

Grey looked at Rachel's flushed face and cleared his throat.

"Well, that we don't know yet. Henrietta, Rebecca, help Mercy to look everywhere in this room. See if it has fallen under the bed or the chest over there."

"How could it have done so? I told you I had put it away."

"Nevertheless, a search must be made."

They searched for some twenty minutes, but there was no sign of the ring. Grey straightened his jacket, his face serious.

"Then there is only one thing left to do."

"And what is that, pray?"

"We must search everyone's room."

"Father!"

"Sir, you cannot mean it!"

"Arthur!"

Grey listened to the shocked reaction of Henrietta, Sidney and his wife, nodding his head firmly.

"There is no choice. Someone must have taken it. We will start with the servants' rooms. Cook's first, and then yours, Aggie."

Aggie's face was scarlet, her eyes brimming with tears.

"Sir, I swear I 'ad nothin' to do with this. I 'aven't taken the mistress's ring."

"I am sure you haven't, but that is easily proved. Come,

girl, lead the way. The sooner we look the sooner your mind will be put at rest."

The others followed silently, rather shaken by Grey's decision. Sara went up the stairs with Sidney, who looked unhappy and guilty.

"Do you think we ought to do this Sara? Search other people's rooms, I mean. It shews we don't trust them."

She shook her head. "I don't know, but what else is there to do? I'm sure we won't find it anywhere, so that no one will be hurt."

"I don't want anyone looking amongst my things." Sidney's pale brown eyes were resentful. "My room is my private place."

"Never mind, it won't take long. Mine will be searched too, you know."

"That is silly. Why should father think you took the ring?"

"I don't think he does. He simply feels we must look everywhere."

Mrs. Tamworth's cold little room produced nothing more startling than an ample supply of corn-plasters, a bottle of cough syrup, and a miscellany of warm flannel petticoats. When Aggie's possessions had been turned over, revealing nothing more sinister than a small pot of rouge amidst her underwear, she stopped crying as they turned to Jenny's corner of the room.

Sara gave Jenny a comforting smile. Sidney was right. It was hateful to have one's belongings pawed over by alien hands, and she could see the distaste in Jenny's face as Arthur opened the first drawer. She was ready to move to the door, when Grey suddenly stopped, his hand poised over Jenny's stockings and scarves.

"What is this?" His voice was very cold, and as he turned to look at Jenny, Sara could see the angry accusation in his eyes. "What does this mean?"

They all stared at him as he picked up the ring, watching the diamonds wink in the light of the oil-lamp which had been lit. Sara looked quickly at Jenny, seeing horror and amazement fight with panic as her colour fled.

"Sir . . . sir . . . I don't know. I swear I don't know! I didn't put it there."

"Who else would do so?"

"I . . . I . . . don't know, sir. But I didn't take it. Oh, sir, I swear I didn't take it!"

Sara took a step towards Jenny, but Grey checked her with a gesture of his hand.

"Stay where you are, Sara, if you please."

"But, uncle, I. . . ."

"Be quiet, I say." Grey turned back to Jenny, who was now weeping hopelessly. "Do not make things worse by lying. It is quite obvious that you did take the ring. Why else should it be in your drawer?"

"Uncle." Sara made one last effort to save Jenny, although she could tell by Grey's face that her task was doomed. "Uncle, I am sure Jenny did not take the ring. She would never do such a thing."

Grey's lips tightened.

"Sara, I have bidden you to be quiet. I am well aware that you and this girl have had more to do with one another than is proper. I have not liked what I have seen, but until now I have not interfered. It is clear that I should have done so, for she has had her head turned by your kindness, which was no kindness at all. Servants should be kept in their place. If they are not, this sort of thing can happen only too easily. Now, it is simply a matter of whether or not to call the police."

"No!"

Grey ignored Sara, his brows bent in a frown as he watched the dejected Jenny sobbing her heart out. Finally, he said slowly:

"I think perhaps not. It is an unpleasant business, and we do not want a fuss made. You are lucky, my girl, this once. You will leave this house within the hour, and I never want to see you again. Do not look to Mrs. Grey to furnish you with a reference, for that you will not get. I doubt that you will get a job easily without one, so your punishment will be severe enough. Now get your things together and be off with you."

He waved the others out of the room, including Sara. She would like to have stayed to help Jenny; to whisper to her that she did not believe her a thief, but Grey was standing in the doorway, his face forbidding, and she had no choice but to go to her own room and sit on the bed to consider what had happened.

Jenny was not a thief. Whoever had taken the ring, it was not Jenny; she was as sure of that as she had ever been of anything. And now Jenny would go. Soon she would hear her creep downstairs to the basement, where, under the accusing eye of Mrs. Tamworth and the blank stare of Aggie, she would leave the house, her small bundle of possessions clutched in her hand.

She could not bear to think what would happen to Jenny with no money and no prospects of another position. She wanted to scream aloud at the injustice of it all. Instead, her thoughts turned back to herself. Once Jenny was gone, there would be no one to whom she could talk freely. Jenny had been her friend; she had helped her to reach Blaise Westerbrook. She had hoped to engage Jenny's assistance in finding the nurse who had looked after her grandfather, but now she would have to do it alone.

Whoever had taken the ring from Aunt Rachel's jewel-case and hidden it in Jenny's drawer had robbed her of her only real friend in No: 11, Candle Square. Sara buried her face in her hands, thinking of the trivial, unpleasant incidents which were beginning to mount up into something much bigger and much more fearful.

For the first time in years, Sara Lessingham was really afraid.

When Blaise Westerbrook's maid informed Candace Martin that her master was giving a ball to which Arthur Grey and his family had been invited, she felt the rage run through her body like a fever.

Westerbrook had lied when he said he did not expect to see his beautiful visitor again. By now Candace had learned the girl's name, and that Blaise had called on her uncle, Arthur Grey. She had also found out, quite by chance, that Grey and Mr. Brown were one and the same person.

She did not know why she felt the girl who lived in Candle Square was such a threat. She knew Blaise had had other women and although she had been jealous of them, they had never really bothered her, but somehow Sara Lessingham was different. She sensed that Blaise thought Sara different too, and her unhappiness increased until it lay like a dead weight in her heart.

It was nearly ten o'clock, and at midnight Arthur Grey, still calling himself Mr. Brown, was coming to call on her.

He had been generous in the past, and was still very passionate. Now she knew that he was Sara Lessingham's uncle, he would find he had to be more generous still if he were to keep his mistress's favours. She smiled thinly to herself. There were a number of unpaid bills to be dealt with. Arthur Grey would be allowed to pay them for her. It would cost him quite a bit, but that was the price he had to pay for getting into her bed, and after all, it was not the same as it was with Blaise. She wasn't in the least in love with Arthur Grey.

By eight o'clock on the 9th December, Sara and her cousins were almost ready for Blaise Westerbrook's ball. They were dressing in Henrietta's room, for hers was the largest and favoured with a coal-fire.

Everyone was helping, from Mercy Thorne to Maud Grimpley, the new under-housemaid who had taken Jenny's place. Maud was slow but very pretty.

Henrietta looked almost attractive that night in a rose taffetta gown. She wore her hair in ringlets for once, and the excitement had touched her cheeks with an unusual pinkness.

Rebecca was in pale blue satin, off the shoulder, trimmed with rows and rows of fine lace. She was in high spirits, turning and twisting about as Mercy tried to fasten the flowers in her hair.

Sara was excited too, although she took care not to let anyone see it. Uncle Arthur had not been entirely happy about the invitation.

'You realise, of course, that Lord Westerbrook is merely being polite," he had said, eyeing her meditatively. "You are the grandchild of an old friend of his father's, and so he conceives it as his duty to recognise the fact. But it is no more than a courtesy."

"Of course, uncle." She had been very careful not to let herself imagine it was more than that, although the possibility that it might have been something other than convention made her heart pump like a steam engine. "I understand that."

"Your aunt does not feel well enough to attend." Arthur had gone on. "But Sidney and I will escort you and the girls. It will be a pleasant experience for you, but you must not expect Westerbrook to concern himself with you after that. His duty will have been done."

Sara looked at herself in the long mirror and wondered what Blaise would make of her dress. It was cream silk, very fine and cunningly draped over her hips, falling rather daringly off the shoulders where it met a swathe of delicate lace. Sara half-smiled to herself when she saw the flush in her cheeks and the deeper rose of her mouth. She had been determined to put her fears behind her for the evening, and not to let Blaise think she was a poor, timid creature afraid of her own shadow.

When they arrived at Eaton Square the house was a blaze of light. There were flowers everywhere, and a host of servants handing round glasses of champagne. Musicians played soft melodies from a specially erected dais.

There was dancing in the drawing-room upstairs, and Sara and her cousins watched in awe as the fashionable ladies and their escorts whirled and turned to the sound of the waltz.

Blaise was a punctilious host and had soon introduced them to a number of people before leaving them again to greet other guests. It was not until the buffet supper began that Sara had the chance to talk to him. Tables had been set in an adjoining salon, glittering with silver and glass, coloured by exquisite flower arrangements and warmed by candles in heavy gold holders.

Sara thought she had never before seen so much food all in one place, nor anything quite so exotic and unreal. She was too overcome to eat much, and she was beginning to realise how alien Blaise's world was from her own, and how foolish and ignorant she had been even to think that he might be aware of her amidst the bevy of duchesses, countesses, and ladies of title and high-rank.

When she found him at her elbow, she became even more confused, blushing in spite of her efforts to remain cool and poised. She tried hard not to look at him, because she was afraid he might see something in her eyes which she was endeavouring to hide.

"Are you enjoying it, Miss Lessingham?"

She smiled quickly, refusing to dwell on the clearness of his eyes or the bold, hard line of his mouth.

"Very much. It was good of you to ask us. I have never been to such a ball before. There are so many here."

"Alas, yes."

"Alas?" She did turn to him then, puzzled by the boredom in his voice. "You sound as though you wish your guests had not come."

"So I do." His smile took the sting out of the words. "I give parties and balls because it is expected of me. It is a duty, no more."

A duty. Sara felt as though Blaise had slapped her. Uncle Arthur had been right; Blaise was fulfilling what he saw as a social obligation, nothing more. It hurt more than she had expected it to do and she turned her head away again in case he should notice it.

"I see."

He gave a soft laugh. "I doubt if you do. I would much prefer to take supper with you, than exchange polite inconsequences with a regiment like this."

He saw her eyes widen and his amusement increased.

"You seem surprised. I suppose someone has told you that I am a wild character, dissipating my health and money in an endless round of pleasures and unmentionable vices."

"No, of course not."

She said it too rapidly and he laughed again.

"You don't lie very well, Sara Lessingham, but no matter. I can assure you that the social round does not appeal to me nearly as much as my friends think it does, or my enemies either, for that matter. What do you like to do?"

She hesitated. "I am not a very interesting person, I'm afraid. My life is a quiet one."

"It didn't sound as though it was particularly quiet from what you told me of it a while ago. Has anything else happened to frighten you?"

Sara looked down at her glass and he saw the dark lashes lie like delicate fans on the pale, alabaster skin. He would have liked to tilt her chin to make her look at him again, but that would have been noticed and talked of by half of London on the following morning.

"No." She tried to smile. "Nothing else. I was wrong and foolish to have bothered you. If I had known...."

"That I was not my father, you wouldn't have come? I'm glad you did. Are you sure nothing else has happened?"

"Quite sure."

She said it firmly, refusing to weaken. He saw the determination, and the lie, but decided not to press her.

"Very well. Then tell me what you like to do."

Glad to be able to turn from the discomfort of his former questions, she said lightly:

"I like to read books."

"Do you now?" He raised an enquiring eyebrow. "What

kind of books?"

"Anything I can get hold of. I've read most of those in Uncle Arthur's library."

"How very diligent of you."

"Not diligent, I just wanted to know more about everything and that was the only way I could learn. I longed to go to school; even to college. Uncle Arthur would not let me, and I had to make do with a governess. In the end I knew more than she did, poor Amy."

"Poor Amy indeed. You must have been a disconcerting pupil. Why did you have this longing to learn?"

"Because I wanted to do something worthwhile with my life. You would not understand, Lord Westerbrook, how dull it is to sit day after day embroidering and sewing and taking tea. I wanted to do something which mattered to other people."

"Beautiful women seldom need to be useful."

She looked at him reproachfully.

"You are laughing at me."

"Not in the least. I merely said that there was no cause for you to be useful, since you are already beautiful."

She smiled tentatively, but then she became serious again.

"But I want to be of use. I cannot conceive that a life spent in stitching beads on to pieces of velvet is fulfilling God's purpose for me."

"There is more than embroidery, surely?" He wasn't laughing now. He was considering the line of her throat, the gentle slope of her shoulders, and the heart-stopping swell of her small breasts under their silk and lace covering. "There is marriage, children; the support and comfort of your husband."

Her face grew blank, the animation dying away as if a light had gone out inside her. He frowned slightly, wondering what made her look as she did.

"Yes, I suppose so, but how many men would want a wife who preferred Homer to a cookery book? A woman who would rather travel round the world, than listen to gossip over the teacups. If you were honest, Lord Westerbrook, you would say none. Only the very brave of us escape; women like Miss Nightingale. But I do not have the courage."

"Perhaps you will not need it."

"I do, I do! I need her courage now, simply to. . . ."

"To what?"

"It is nothing."

He raised his hand to take hers, regardless of what would be whispered the next morning, but before he had the chance to touch her, he was hailed by a group of his friends and regretfully made his excuses to Sara, cursing to himself as he was drawn away.

Sara had no time to rue his departure, for Sidney was there, claiming the next dance.

"You look so lovely, Sara."

He said it earnestly, squeezing her hand as they moved into the next room where the music had started again.

"Thank you, Sidney."

She said it absently, most of her mind still on Blaise Westerbrook.

"Sometimes I think you don't even see me, Sara. When you look at me, you seem to stare right through me."

She came to earth with a jolt, meeting Sidney's hurt brown eyes with her own.

"I . . . I . . . didn't mean to do that." She was genuinely sorry, for she was fond of Sidney. "I think I may have drunk too much."

He gave a forgiving chuckle.

"That's all right then. I wouldn't want you not to see me. Sara."

"Mm?"

"You know that father . . . well . . . that father wants us to marry?"

She felt herself grow cold, wishing that she could release herself from Sidney's hold and rush off the floor, but she could not run away every time the subject was mentioned, and it was clear that Uncle Arthur was a long way from finishing with the matter."

"Yes, I know."

"I'm not asking you to say yes straight away. I know I'm a very ordinary person, not like Oliver at all."

"I'm just as fond of you as I was of Oliver."

"Are you?" His face lit up for a moment like an eager child's. "Oh, I'm so glad. I wasn't sure you see. Oliver was so . . . well . . . Oliver was different."

"You miss him, Sidney, don't you?"

"Of course, don't you?"

"Yes, of course. Uncle Arthur does too."

"I know." The young face puckered with something which made Sara want to weep. "Oliver was special to him, you see. I wish he'd talk about him, but he won't. I think it would be easier to . . . well . . . it would be easier if we could speak about him now and again."

"We can, when we are alone."

His face brightened again. "Oh yes! We could do that, couldn't we? It wouldn't seem so final then, would it?"

The dance was finished and the floor was clearing. Grey came up to them, nodding his approval at Sara, beaming at Sidney's flushed face.

"Time to go, my dears, the carriage is here. Come and thank your host and then we must be on our way. Ah, here are Henrietta and Rebecca. Good; have you enjoyed it?"

He herded them towards Westerbrook, who bade them farewell with a graceful bow and a handshake for Grey. He hardly looked at Sara, and it was more than the powdering of snow which greeted them outside which made her shiver. He had almost ignored her; as if he had never seen her before.

When they got home Rebecca went to her mother's room to tell her all about the ball, whilst Mercy helped Sara to remove her dress and to unpin her hair.

"I hope it won't turn your head," said Mercy bluntly. "I'm not sure that Arthur was wise to let any of you go. It's very unsettling."

"I didn't find it so," replied Sara untruthfully. "It was a beautiful house, Mercy. So large, with lovely paintings and silver, and wonderful furniture."

"And now you've come back to Candle Square." Mercy's lips were compressed. "That's not your world; you'll never move in those circles, so what is the use of shewing you something which you can never have?"

Sara sat at the dressing-table and began to brush her hair, but Mercy took the brush from her and began the steady downward strokes. "Time you got down to realities, my girl."

"And what are realities?"

"Marriage, of course. A home and children."

"Marriage?"

"Yes, marriage to someone steady and reliable, who could look after you. Someone like Matthew."

Sara raised her head and met Mercy's eyes in the mirror. "Have you told Uncle Arthur what you think, Mercy?"

The red on Mercy's gaunt cheeks was ugly and she laid the brush down with a loud click.

"No, I haven't, but you think about it. You need someone to look after you, don't you? It's not everyone who'd want to...."

She broke off and picked up Sara's evening shoes.

"Well, never mind that now. It's late, and I must get downstairs. I've a hundred things to do before I can go to bed."

She went out without another word, and Sara stared at the reflection of the empty room behind her. So many people seemed to think she needed to be looked after. First Uncle Arthur, who wanted her to marry Sidney now that Oliver was no longer there; Sidney himself, and now Mercy, who pressed the suit of Matthew, her nephew. Even Blaise had mentioned marriage as the sensible solution to her future.

Wearily she got up and undressed and hopped into bed before the icy draughts could freeze her toes. She blew out the candles and lay back, waiting for the house to settle down to sleep. She dozed for a while but then suddenly she awoke with a start, as she heard the familiar creaks begin.

When the stairs were quiet again, she huddled under the bedclothes shutting her eyes and ears to what was going on beyond her door. She would not think about it. She would think about Blaise instead, remembering him as he had stood talking to her amidst the galaxy of lights, the perfume of the flowers and the gay merriment of music and voices.

When she fell asleep again she began to dream, not of Blaise Westerbrook and his ball in Eaton Square, but of fire. Fire which encircled the face of her mother, turning it brown at the edges, creeping over it until it crinkled up like a piece of charred paper as the screams from the distorted mouth died way into silence.

Sara went to the shops in Kensington High Street the next morning. Maud Grimpley went with her, holding the basket and the list. Sara found that she missed Jenny unbearably, still bitter that the girl had been accused of something she had not done. She wished that there was some way of getting in touch with her, so that she could give her a little money. The thought that Jenny might be homeless, perhaps even hungry, was too agonising a thing to dwell on for long, but Maud was amiable enough. She had thick fair hair and sleepy blue eyes under heavy lids, a small turned-up nose and a wide, sensuous mouth.

When they had been to Mudie's Library for Rachel, and purchased some cottons and needles for Mercy, they crossed the road to buy a box of chocolates for Mrs. Tamworth, who had a birthday on the following day. There were hot rolls to collect from Bailey's, and the latest issue of the *Ladies' Gazette* for Rebecca, and then they turned homeward again.

Mrs. Tamworth was out in the area, sweeping up some fallen leaves. She called out to Maud to hurry up, beckoning the girl down the narrow iron steps and hustling her inside. Sara had her foot on the first of the steps leading to the front door when she saw something out of the corner of her eye and turned quickly.

The old woman whom she had seen from her window was standing not more than a few feet away from her. She was in black, as before, bunched and shapeless in a straggling shawl with wisps of grey hair poking out from underneath an old-fashioned bonnet.

Sara fought down the impulse to run up the steps and ring the door-bell. It was too silly to be afraid of an old woman whom she did not know. She tried to smile.

"Did you ... did you want to see someone?"

She managed to get some words out at last, drawing back in alarm as the woman began to curse and shake her fist. Sara could see the venom in her, shuddering as the swearing mounted to shouts. Then she turned and fled, hammering on the door until Aggie opened it, her eyes popping with surprise.

"Is something wrong, Miss Sara?"

Sara leaned against the wall, waiting until her heart had slowed down before she nodded.

"That old woman out there. She cursed me; it was horrible."

"Old woman?"

Aggie poked her head out of the door.

"I don't see no old woman."

"She's there though. I have just seen her."

Aggie went down the steps, looking up and down the street and finally returning to shake her head.

"No woman there, Miss Sara. No one in sight, in fact."

"There must be. She was there a moment ago."

"Not now, miss. No sign of anyone."

Aggie closed the door firmly. It was too cold to stand there arguing, and now Miss Thorne was advancing along the passage to enquire what was wrong.

"Miss Sara said she saw an old woman, miss." Aggie's eyes were sly. "No one there, of course. Said she cursed her."

"What are you talking about, Aggie?" Mercy was tart. "What do you mean?"

"I saw an old woman." Sara could feel the disbelief in the others. It hung about her like a pall. "She cursed me and shook her fist at me."

"But she weren't there when I went to see." Aggie smirked. "No one in sight, miss, as I said."

"Go downstairs, Aggie," said Mercy. "You've got plenty to do in the kitchen, so go and get on with it. Sara, you'd better go and lie down. Perhaps I ought to call Dr. Blackmore."

"What for?" Sara's voice was taut. "I'm not ill. I tell you there was someone outside."

"Aggie doesn't think so. Now be a good girl and go and lie down and I'll get Maud to bring you up some tea. We mustn't take any chances with you, must we? The doctor said you might have to rest more, if. . . ."

"If what? If what, Mercy?"

"If you didn't get any better, my dear. Now off you go. I'll send the tea up in a minute."

Drearily Sara obeyed. Had the old woman really been there after all? Aggie Lowther said not, and why should she lie? Mercy obviously didn't think so either. It was terrifying not to know whether the things which were happening round one were real or only in one's own imagination.

She bit her lip, tears starting to her eyes. There was no way to be certain, of course, that was the problem. She would have to be careful. If she grew too wild in her insistence that things were happening, when everyone else knew that they were not, they would send for Dr. Blackmore, and perhaps other doctors as well.

SEVEN

On a dull Sunday morning in mid-December, No : 11 Candle Square awoke to find a north-east wind blowing gustily round the house, and that Aggie Lowther, its parlour maid, had disappeared.

It took some time to establish the second fact, for there were so many places where Aggie could have been, busy about her work, that it was not until breakfast was ready that the truth was borne in upon the household.

Mrs. Tamworth emerged from the basement to serve the meal herself, for she could not bring herself to trust Maud Grimpley to do it properly.

Mercy Thorne frowned. It was Aggie's place to bring in the tea and coffee, and she said so sharply.

"I know that, miss. But 'ow she's goin' to bring hup the tray when she's not 'ere, I'm sure I don't know."

"Not here?"

"That's right, not 'ere. There's no sign of 'er."

Arthur Grey lowered his newspaper and considered Mrs. Tamworth thoughtfully.

"You mean she's not in the house?"

"No, sir, she's not. We've looked all over."

"Then she must have gone out for something."

"I can't think what, sir, and when we found she'd gone, the bolts on the front door 'adn't been drawn, nor those down below neither."

"How very extraordinary." Grey cleared his throat. "Mrs. Tamworth, you can't have looked properly."

"I assure you we 'ave, sir. She's not 'ere, and that's a fact."

"Are her things still here?"

"Things, miss? I don't know what you mean."

"It's simple enough," snapped Mercy. "The girl's baggage; is it still here?"

"I 'aven't looked."

"Then do so at once and let me know what you find."

Mrs. Tamworth stumped off, returning in ten minutes to announce that there was nothing belonging to Aggie left in the room which she shared with Maud.

"Then she's packed her bags and gone." Grey rose from the table and wiped his moustache carefully. "She must have left during the night. Didn't the other wench, what's her name, hear her go?"

"Maud, sir? No, I asked 'er. She sleeps 'eavy, of course, but she didn't 'ear nothing."

Grey shrugged. "Well, that's that. We won't see her again. Girls like her do go off sometimes without warning. Some man no doubt. Miss Thorne will get in touch with the agency to-morrow; you'll have to manage for to-day, Mrs. Tamworth. Mercy, I'll have another cup of coffee in my study, if you please. I've things to do before church."

Sara finished her own coffee and rose too. She had slept badly again and there were dark smudges under her eyes. She had played with her food, trying not to let Sidney, Rebecca and Mercy notice that she was not eating, for she could not face questions at the moment. She felt strung-up and nervous, as if poised for some disaster; not sure of herself any more.

Rebecca chuckled. "I expect papa's right. She's run away with her lover."

Sidney looked vague. "Her lover? Did Aggie have a lover?"

"Certain to have done. Mama always said she was a trollop, didn't she, Mercy?"

"I've no idea, and I've far too much to do to stay here gossiping. Hurry up and finish your breakfast, Rebecca; Maud must clear in five minutes."

They watched her go and Rebecca sniggered again.

"I expect Mercy's jealous. She's never had a lover."

"You don't know that Aggie had either." Sidney was trying to be fair. "There might have been some other reason why she went."

Rebecca was scornful, popping the last piece of toast and marmalade into her mouth.

"What could there be? You're so stupid, Sidney, you won't see what is under your nose."

"I don't think she has gone."

Sidney and Rebecca turned to stare at Sara, and she flushed.

"I . . . I . . . that is . . . I think she is still here."

"Oh, Sara, really! How could she be? The house has been searched, hasn't it?"

"I didn't hear her go out last night."

"What does that signify? She would have gone quietly."

"I was awake. I'm sure I would have heard her."

"Well, you didn't, and you'd better not let father or Mercy hear you say such things. They'd think you were being . . . well . . . being peculiar again."

Sara's colour burned deeper and she said no more, but later that day, in the afternoon when the household was taking its Sunday nap, she came out of her room and stood for a while in the passage. She had no idea why she was so sure that Aggie hadn't left the house. It wasn't simply that Mrs. Tamworth had said the bolts had not been drawn; there was a basement window which Aggie could have used if she had been determined enough. Her belief was not as rational as that, and she could feel herself shaking. Perhaps Rebecca was right; perhaps she was being peculiar again.

Yet the feeling was too strong to shrug off, and after a while she walked to the foot of the steps leading up to the top floor. She realised then that she had never been to the top attics, not even in childhood when she and her cousins had played hide-and-seek. Somehow she had always managed to avoid that part of the house.

Now she took a deep breath and began to mount them.

It was icy cold and the light was not good. She wished she had thought to bring a candle, particularly as when her foot touched the third stair the familiar creaking began and made her heart jump into her mouth.

Somehow she got to the top landing, a small, dusty square with four closed doors on one side of it. The attic did not cover the whole of the house, simply the west side, and she was glad that there was nothing behind her back as she turned to open the first door. It was a black hole, but she could tell there was nothing inside but trunks, baskets and valises. The second room was locked and the third was small and crammed with old furniture, and discarded vases and ornaments.

When she opened the fourth door she felt a sudden sense of dread. There was enough light from the tiny window to bring the room into focus, and she saw the torn curtains at the window, the threadbare rug on the floor, the bed and chair, and a chest of drawers. She moved closer to the bed, reluctant to leave the safety of the doorway and a possible escape, but drawn by the sight of the blankets and rumpled sheets. The pillow still bore the indentation of a human head, and a cheap satin wrap smelling of inexpensive scent was thrown over the foot.

Someone had slept there, and probably not long ago. But who, and why? Sara turned and fled.

Later, when she was more composed, she mentioned the matter to Rachel and Mercy Thorne as they took tea together in Rachel's room.

"Really, Sara." Rachel was irritable. "You're talking nonsense! There may be a bed up there, but no one could have slept in it."

"I saw the sheets and blankets, and a woman's wrap."

"Impossible. You really will have to . . . well . . . you'll have to learn to be careful what you say. People will think. . . ."

"That I'm not normal." Sara said it dully, seeing their total disbelief. "But it's the truth, Aunt Rachel. I did see these things. Someone had been there."

"I'll go up myself," said Mercy and put her plate down. "Come with me, Sara, and we'll put an end to this straight away."

They left Rachel and went upstairs. In the attics it was as silent as a tomb, save, of course, for the complaining of the wood as Mercy and Sara mounted the stairs.

"Now shew me. Which room is it?"

Sara moved past Mercy and opened the door, stopping dead as the room came to life again in the light of her candle. The bed was still there, but there were no blankets or sheets; no pillows or wrap. Simply a horsehair mattress folded up in a great roll, exposing the rusting iron springs and a quantity of dust.

Mercy turned to the door.

"Come downstairs, Sara, it's too cold to stay up here. Come along, and I'll pour you a nice hot cup of tea to warm you up."

The kindness was rare and more terrifying than anger would have been. Sara felt limp as she trailed downstairs again. A rousing scolding for leading Mercy on a wild goose chase would have been reassuring; then she would have known that Mercy thought her responsible for her own actions. The patient acceptance of her bizarre behaviour sent chills down Sara's spine.

"No, there was nothing," Mercy answered Rachel's question in an expressionless tone, "but it is dark up there, and imagination can play tricks on one."

"Not on me." Rachel glared at Sara. "I hope that I haven't reached the stage where I see things, which aren't there."

Mercy turned the conversation in a different direction, and finally the awful tea-party came to an end. Sara crept up to her own room and sat on the bed, pulling a warm shawl about her shoulders. So she was imagining things, after all. There hadn't been anything up in the attic except the bare bones of old furniture; she had been day-dreaming again. There were no sheets and pillows, no shiny satin wrap, yet they had seemed so real; so solid.

She had to face facts now, for no one could have moved the things in time. She sat stunned, wishing she had not involved Blaise Westerbrook in her problems, yet yearning illogically, for a sight of him. If he were here now, he would be able to coax her out of her depression, laughing at her for making a fuss because she thought she had seen something in the half-light which wasn't there.

She went to bed early that night. She still had the feeling that Aggie Lowther was in the house. She knew it was absurd, because there was no corner in which the girl could have hidden, and why should she be hiding in any event? She would have to learn to control such wild notions, particularly now that she knew she could no longer rely on her own judgment. Aggie had gone off with her unknown admirer, sneaking through the basement window at the dead of night; it was as simple as that.

She slept very heavily and without dreaming, lying like one dead until eight o'clock the next morning when Maud came to pull the curtains back and to announce that it was snowing. Sara's eyelids were so heavy that she could hardly raise them, and she felt as though she were drifting off to sleep again in spite of her efforts to rouse herself.

Then Maud gave a sharp cry and Sara jerked into wakefulness.

"What is it?" She tried to sit up, feeling her body aching as if she had been beaten. "Whatever is the matter, Maud?"

Maud had moved round to the other side of the bed, the teacup rattling in her shaking hand, her face pale in the dull morning light.

"Th . . . there . . . miss! Oh, Miss Sara, what've you been doin'?"

Sara glanced down, following Maud's eyes, her lips parting in disbelief as she saw the open razor lying close to her hand. Then slowly she raised her arm and looked at her wrist with the fine red line where the blade had just skimmed the surface of the skin.

She went on staring at the tell-tale mark in numb silence as Maud dropped the teacup with a clatter and turned and fled from the room.

Three days later Sara Lessingham agreed to marry her cousin Sidney. She sat in Arthur Grey's study, pale and forlorn. Everyone had been so kind. After Maud's startling announcement, no one had been shocked by what had happened. They had treated her as an invalid, to be coddled and loved, even Aunt Rachel's tongue stilled.

"My dear." Grey sat on the opposite side of the hearth and regarded her with concern. "I don't want to burden you at such a time as this, but you will realise that something must be done."

She nodded without speaking.

"You still have no recollection of taking the razor?" His voice was very gentle. "I wondered perhaps if something. . . ."

"No, uncle, I remember nothing except falling asleep. I didn't even dream that night."

"Mm." He still looked grave. "Then it may be that you were. . . ."

"Were what?"

"Walking in your sleep."

She nodded again. He was probably right. What other explanation was there?

"Have you thought any more of what I said to you, Sara; about Sidney, I mean?"

She swallowed hard. "I . . . I . . . no, not really."

"I think you should." He coughed, finding it difficult to choose the right words. "We have got to decide what to do, you see. I am so very fond of you, my dear, you know that. I wouldn't want you to . . . well . . . to have to go away. I feel, and Rachel agrees with me, that if you were to lead a normal married life you would improve. You would have many things to occupy your mind, and you'd soon get over these ... fancies. You and Sidney could stay here at first, of course, but soon he'll be in a position to set up his own establishment. I'd help, naturally."

"And if I didn't marry Sidney?"

He shrugged, looking more uncomfortable than ever.

"Then we'd have to see if we could find some nice nursing home somewhere. You need help, Sara."

"But what if marriage does not cure me?"

"It will, m'dear, it will." He was briskly reassuring. "You've been alone too much; had too much time to think and remember the past. Put it all behind you and start afresh, that's the thing to do."

She considered the fire for a long moment, watching the flames leap up into the darkened chimney. It had all started with a fire, of course. Not a small, decently contained fire like this, but with a raging furnace which had swept away her life and left it in ashes.

"Very well." She had not meant to agree so quickly, but now it was done. She felt no particular emotion; just a sense of inevitability. For a brief second she thought about Blaise Westerbrook, but that was ridiculous. Even if she had been normal, he would not have been interested in her. "Very well, uncle, if you think it would be for the best, I will marry Sidney."

Arthur Grey gave a deep sigh, his smile warming her and enfolding her in its pleasure.

"Dear Sara, I'm so glad. It is a wise decision and you will not regret it. I cannot tell you how deep is my sense of relief. It would have broken my heart if you had had to go away."

Later, Sidney found her in the sitting-room, waiting for Rachel and Mercy. He came over to her quickly and sat beside her on the sofa.

"Father has told me that you have agreed." He blushed. "You know how pleased I am, don't you, Sara?"

She gave him a faint smile, trying to envisage him as a husband and lover, but seeing him only as the small boy who had played cricket with her on hot summer afternoons.

"Yes, Sidney."

"I know you don't love me, at least not that way." His colour deepened and he avoided her eye. "But I will cherish you, Sara, I promise."

She tried to smile again. Perhaps it would be a comfort to have Sidney to cherish her, as he put it. Perhaps Uncle Arthur had been right; maybe she had been alone too much. She had never felt any real warmth for Henrietta or Rebecca, and certainly none for Aunt Rachel. Even her links with her grandfather were tenuous, for she had been unable to trace the nurse of whom Victoria Roseby had spoken. Her mother and father were dead, and Blaise. . . . She forced herself to stop thinking of Westerbrook.

"Do you love me, Sidney; like that, I mean?"

Sidney hesitated.

"You are beautiful and gentle."

"That is no answer."

He looked uncertain.

"I know, but it is all I can tell you. I don't know whether I love you like some men love women. I don't really know what being in love means. Of course I care for you, you know that, and I'm proud of you because you are cleverer than most girls I know. Do you think that will be enough?"

He glanced at her anxiously and she felt a tremor go through her.

"I don't know, but we'll have to make the best of it, won't we?"

She looked back at the fire, feeling the tears very close. If she had been going to marry Blaise, there would have been no question of making the best of it. He would know what it was like to be in love. She knew too; from the moment that she had first seen him she had known. It would make it that much harder to live with Sidney, but the die was cast now.

Blaise had his own life to live, and he would probably be relieved to hear of her betrothal because he would no longer have to concern himself about her problems. They were Sidney's responsibility now.

"We'll live here for a while, did father tell you?"

"Yes."

Even that avenue of escape was closed to her for the time being. She would still have to stay in the house in Candle Square with its stairs which made noises and its attic where mysterious things happened. It might be years before Sidney could afford a house of his own.

"You do want to marry me, don't you? It wasn't simply that father persuaded you because . . . because. . . ."

He could not go on, sitting silently as the ugly truth hung between them. Then Sara forced herself to speak. She could not make Sidney suffer because of her.

"No, no, it wasn't that. I do want to marry you, Sidney, and I'll try to make you a good wife."

The lie nearly choked her, but Sidney was happier, smiling as he bent over to kiss her lightly on the cheek.

"My congratulations, Miss Lessingham."

Blaise Westerbrook said it coolly, finishing his coffee without haste.

Arthur Grey was very cheerful that morning, glad to welcome Westerbrook and to make his proud announcement.

"Yes, we are all very happy," he said and beamed at Sara. "It is something which has been near to my heart for some time."

"Indeed?"

Blaise studied Sara's face. She looked thinner and her eyes were haunted. If Arthur Grey was happy, Sara Lessingham certainly was not.

"Oh yes, they are very fond of each other; it is a most excellent arrangement." He took Westerbrook's cup and handed it to Henrietta. "More coffee for our visitor, m'dear."

"And when is the wedding to take place?"

"Some time in January."

Blaise's eyebrows rose slowly as he switched his attention from Sara to Grey.

"So soon?"

"There is no reason to wait." Grey was brisk, giving Sara a loving smile. "They will live here, you see, so there's nothing much to get ready. Later on, we'll see about a house for them, but there's no hurry."

Sara stirred her coffee and stole a look at Blaise. It had been an unpleasant surprise when Laura Higgins, the new parlour maid, had announced Westerbrook's arrival. She had not expected to see him again, and the sight of his face shattered the fragile peace of mind she had tried so hard to husband since her decision had been made. Clearly, he thought the engagement a trifle unusual, but then he had no way of knowing why she had acquiesced.

"They will have a short honeymoon in Bournemouth, and by then we shall have rearranged the spare room for them. It will all work out very well."

Blaise caught Sara's eye and for a moment it seemed that they were alone in the room. She thought Blaise must be laughing at her for accepting Bournemouth when she had longed to travel round the world; it was such a shabby compromise. Westerbrook, however, was not thinking of Bournemouth at all. He was contemplating with distaste the notion of her sharing the refurbished spare room with the gangling Sidney Grey.

When he had gone, Sara remained in the morning-room with Henrietta, trying to work on a cover for a footstool. When Laura brought the letters in she took hers thankfully, glad to have something to turn her thoughts away from Blaise. Henrietta went off with Rachel's, and Sara read Victoria Roseby's latest epistle. When Sara had finished the last page she glanced down at her lap and felt the nape of her neck prickle. She didn't know why she hadn't seen the other envelope straight away, for it was larger than the rest; thick white paper and bold black handwriting demanding to be read.

At first she thought she would throw it straight into the fire without opening it, but something held her back.

The words seemed to jump up and hit her between the eyes, mocking her for her innocence when she did not understand them, smugly satisfied when the accusations and threats made her quiver. The fact that she knew herself to be entirely innocent did not seem to help. The graphic description of her purported sexual activities with Arthur Grey was no less shattering because of its absurdity. It still covered her whole being with a film of mire, making her feel sick with its innuendoes and blatant filth.

Finally, she screwed it up and threw it into the fire.

It was only when she had forced herself to thread her needle again, her heart still thumping unevenly, that the thought struck her and she raised her head quickly. She hadn't imagined the letters, nor had she written them to herself. Even if she had risen in her sleep and somehow got hold of one of Uncle Arthur's razors, and later tried to slash her wrists, she had not taken a pen and written the cruel lies and calumnies which she had just read. That would have been quite beyond her, no matter how abnormal she had become; she simply did not have the knowledge to write such things.

Someone else had done that. Someone close at hand who knew her well, and who hated her; someone malicious and evil and spiteful.

Still stunned, she opened the rest of her letters, hardly seeing them, glad when Laura returned to tell her that Rachel wanted her. She went up the stairs slowly, wishing there was someone she could talk to about the letters, but she knew there was no one. Now that she had destroyed them, no one would believe that they had existed. They would say she had invented them, and would shake their heads in pity or exasperation. She might have been able to tell Blaise, terrible though the missives had been, but Blaise would not call again. She swallowed the painful lump in her throat and went into Rachel's room, closing the door quietly behind her.

"Now, my dear Augustine, let us see where we are."
Westerbrook took a glass of whisky from his valet and lay back in his chair. It was one o'clock in the morning, but Dean was used to late hours, and he was becoming as interested as his master in the goings-on in Candle Square.
"For some reason which is not clear to me, Sara Lessingham has agreed to marry her cousin Sidney."
"You think she has been forced into it, my lord?"
"Yes, but not in the obvious way. There has been no coercion, yet clearly she is unhappy."
"What kind of man is he? The cousin, I mean."
"A harmless enough youth; inexperienced and rather shy. I doubt whether this was his idea."
"Then it must be the uncle's."
"Probably, but why I do not know. But there are other things to consider as well as this mésalliance. First, one of the maids has disappeared."
"Yes, my lord, a girl called Aggie Lowther. Mr. Roper was fortunate enough to strike up an acquaintance with the other servant, Maud, and she was more than ready to talk about it. Not that there's much to tell really. The girl just vanished one night. According to Maud, Arthur Grey says she packed her bags and left."
"Without a word?"
"Precisely so, my lord. There were the other matters too, of course, like the old woman."
"Yes." Blaise was meditative. "And the attic where Sara says she saw signs of someone using a bed, and a woman's dressing-gown."
"Which weren't there, it seems, when Miss Mercy Thorne went to look."
"Someone could have moved the stuff."
"Maud says no one else was in at the time, except herself

and cook in the kitchen, and Mrs. Grey, Miss Thorne and Miss Sara, who were together in Mrs. Grey's bedroom."

"You think Miss Lessingham imagined it?"

"It looks rather as if she did. What other explanation is there?"

Westerbrook gave a faint sigh. "I really don't know, at the moment. What did Arnold Roper have to say to-day?"

Dean hesitated and Blaise said curtly :

"What is it? Why do you look like that? Has something else happened to Sara?"

"No. Well, no, not exactly, my lord."

"For God's sake!"

"It is like this, my lord." Dean hurried on, seeing the anger and fear mingled in his master. "It was only to-day that Maud mentioned it to Roper. Apparently the girl had been afraid to say anything until now, but somehow it slipped out."

"What did?"

"On the morning after Miss Sara thought she saw those things in the attic, Maud took her her morning tea in bed as usual. After she had pulled the curtains and gone round to put the cup down, she saw a razor on the bed."

"What!"

"Yes, my lord, an open razor, but there is more."

Westerbrook's mouth had thinned to a straight line.

"I am sure there is. Go on, what else?"

"There was a mark on one of Miss Sara's wrists, as if she had tried to slash it. A thin pink line, not quite cutting the skin, but it was obvious what had happened."

Blaise finished his whisky and held out the glass.

"Give me another, Augustine, I think I need it. Are you trying to tell me that Sara Lessingham attempted to kill herself?"

"I am only repeating what Arnold Roper told me." Dean filled the glass quickly. "Maud was telling the truth; he was sure of that."

"The truth as she saw it, perhaps."

"My lord?"

"I don't believe Sara tried to commit suicide. Why should she?"

"Perhaps because . . . well . . . that is . . . if she is really. . . ."

"Mad?" Westerbrook gave a short laugh. "Yes, if she were mad she might try, I agree, but I don't concede that she is. Anyone of these incidents I might swallow, but all of them put together makes too indigestible a mouthful for me. No, Augustine, no! I won't accept it."

"Yet it could be no more than a series of coincidences." Dean could see the fierce rejection in his master, yet he felt bound to point out the alternative. "Oliver Grey's death could have been an accident, and the maid could simply have gone off without telling anyone; these girls do sometimes, you know. Compton could have eaten some bad food and the rest could have been in Miss Sara's mind, or things she did without knowing it."

Westerbrook slumped back in his chair and swore under his breath.

"I don't want to believe you, but I am forced to admit you might be right. Every instinct in me tells me that you are wrong yet, without proof, it is hard to deny entirely what you are saying. And if Sara herself believes that she is mad, perhaps that is why she has been persuaded to marry Sidney. Keeping it in the family, as it were, so that no one else will ever know about it. Sidney is to become her keeper."

"It could be that way, my lord."

"And equally it could not." Blaise shut his eyes. "It could be someone else, Augustine, but who? And why? What would anyone have to gain by trying to make Sara Lessingham think she is going out of her mind?"

"Nothing that I can see."

"Nor I, yet if it is someone else there has to be a reason. You said so yourself when she first called here."

"Roper's a good man. He can find no cause."

"No, but perhaps he wouldn't if the person responsible is

clever enough and knows how to cover his, or her, tracks."

"Do you want Roper to continue to watch, my lord?"

"Of course. Tell him to keep asking Maud questions too. I want to know everything that happens in that house until I am sure that Sara is . . . well . . . that there is no one else involved."

"And if there isn't anyone else, my lord?"

Dean's voice was very gentle and Westerbrook shewed his teeth.

"I really don't know at the moment. I'm not ready to consider that possibility yet. Go to bed, Augustine, it's late and I've got a lot to think about."

Christmas that year came decked in snow and frost.

On Christmas night there was a party to celebrate the festival and the engagement of Sara and Sidney, and the drawing-room and dining-room were thrown open to the crowd of friends who came to offer their congratulations and to bring their gifts.

The house was bright with decorations and lights. Everyone semed to be more cheerful, particularly Arthur Grey, who had insisted on the party despite Sara's doubts.

It reminded Sara of her first Christmas at Candle Square, when they had gathered round the big tree and opened the presents with cries of delight. There had been gifts again this morning.

They had all gone to church, joining in the carols as they had done at that earlier Christmastide. The dinner had been just as gargantuan.

Rebecca came up to her and Sara pushed the recollection of that other Christmas away from her, smiling as her cousin did a pirouette to shew off her new dress of pale yellow brocade.

"I wish Matthew could have been here."

"Matthew?"

"Matthew Compton, of course." Rebecca's voice sharpened.

"I suppose you've forgotten him now that papa has made Sidney say he would marry you."

Sara winced. "No, I haven't forgotten him, but I do not see what he has to do with my marrying Sidney."

"I thought you liked him."

"I was not in the least interested in Matthew."

"Nor in Sidney, until papa said you'd have to go away if you didn't have someone to look after you."

"Rebecca! How do you...."

"How do I know what he said?" Rebecca smothered a laugh. "I know most of what goes on in this house. What I don't hear myself, others tell me about. Poor Sara; I can't imagine anything more dull than being married to Sidney. He's such a bore, not a bit like Oliver was. You liked Oliver, didn't you?"

"Of course; he was my cousin."

Sara said it stonily and hoped that Rebecca would go away, but Rebecca was not quite finished.

"I think it was more than that; just being his cousin, I mean. Oliver was very handsome, wasn't he? Wouldn't you have liked to have made love to him?"

"Rebecca!" Sara was shaken. She had not thought her cousin capable of such thoughts, never mind expressing them openly. "That is a dreadful thing to say."

"Are you shocked?" Rebecca smoothed her hair with one hand, shewing her small white teeth in amusement. "Poor innocent Sara. What a lot you have to learn."

When she moved away, Sara felt herself trembling again, angry with herself because everything nowadays seemed to have the power to upset her. Yet she had never heard Rebecca speak like that before and it was disquieting. If Rebecca was capable of such thoughts, and as she clearly disliked her, was she also capable of writing anonymous letters? It would make a terrible kind of sense, for Rebecca was close to her.

She made herself put the dreadful possibility out of her mind as Sidney came up to take her to the dining-room where a buffet supper had been laid out, but later, when he had gone to get her a glass of wine, it came back to her and scratched at her with spiteful claws.

She got up restlessly, moving through the chattering guests, smiling vaguely at one here and there, until she reached the hall. There was a small side window, the curtains not yet drawn, and for a second Sara looked out at the clean stretch of untrodden snow. She was about to turn away when she saw it, and felt every drop of blood drain from her cheeks.

It was a face, at least she supposed it was, for she had never seen anything like it before. It was pale as wax with hollowed sockets where the eyes should have been, festooned with cobwebs as if it had lain in a dusty place for many years. She was vaguely aware that its teeth looked sharp and too long, but then she shut her eyes and began to scream in sheer panic, holding herself upright against the wall until people began to rush towards her exclaiming in alarm.

When the first hum had died down Grey said slowly:

"Now, my dear, it couldn't have been as bad as that." He looked puzzled, watching Sara closely as he patted her hand. "Probably some urchin peering in to watch the party."

"No!" She rejected the explanation with violence. "It wasn't an urchin. It wasn't a human being at all. It couldn't have been! It had no eyes and...."

She knew her voice was rising with hysteria but she couldn't help it. She knew also that the people round her were staring at her, a few with sympathy, some with curiosity, others with something rather like disgust in their eyes.

"It... it... wasn't human."

"But, Sara, my love, what else could it have been? It's all the excitement and fuss that's done it. You're overwrought, that's what it is. Now, we've held the party up long enough. Sidney, Rebecca, take our guests back to the drawing-room. Mercy, help Sara up to her room, and let her lie down for a while."

"There is no need for Mercy to come. Please, Uncle Arthur,

I'm all right alone."

"But...."

"No! I want to be alone. Please!"

"Very well." He exchanged a resigned look with Mercy Thorne. "Mercy will come up later on. Be careful, Sara."

She hardly heard him, hurrying upstairs to her room on the cold second floor. She wanted to cry, but she couldn't. She wanted to scream again, forcing people to listen to her so that she could convince them that she really had seen something outside the window. Something with a face which she would never forget.

She forced her legs to move, getting to the dressing-table somehow to take off her pearl necklace with trembling fingers. Then her eye caught sight of something on the floor and she gave a faint cry.

Her new watch, Sidney's gift, lay smashed in pieces at her feet, the fine gold chain the only whole part left. Slowly she knelt down and picked up the broken fragments, holding them in her hand as the tears began to trickle down her cheeks and the fear which had been circling round her for so long closed in to lock her in its grip.

EIGHT

A fortnight before the wedding, Blaise Westerbrook called at Candle Square. Mercy shewed him into the morning-room, and after a while Arthur Grey appeared with Sara following slowly behind.

"I hope you will forgive the intrusion." Blaise was shaken by Sara's appearance, but he concealed his dismay with commendable self-control. "I wanted to bring my gift myself."

"No intrusion, my lord." Grey was in a very good humour, smiling affably as he waved Blaise to a chair. "We are delighted to see you, and it is most generous of you to think of the young couple. Sidney is not here, of course. He has gone to stay with friends of ours in Chelsea for the next two weeks."

"Of course."

Blaise felt the irritation rise in him. Two weeks sounded very close at hand, and he was still no nearer to a solution of the puzzle than when he had started.

"We did not think to send you an invitation, because we assumed your time would be too fully occupied for our small ceremony, but you would be welcome if you wished to come; very welcome."

"I shall be out of London. Otherwise I would have been glad to have accepted."

Grey nodded and the conversation became general, Sara sitting very still and silent, trying not to look at Blaise, and Westerbrook trying equally hard to concentrate on his host and not to dwell on the almost transparent quality of Sara's skin and the pain he saw in her eyes.

When Laura came to tell Grey that someone had called to

see him on urgent business, he rose and motioned the maid to stay, excusing himself and promising to return as quickly as possible. Blaise waited until the door had closed and a decent interval had elapsed, then he said to Laura :

"I want to speak to Miss Lessingham alone, and I do not want your master to know that I have done so. Can you keep a secret like that?"

Laura grinned knowingly and pocketed the gold sovereign, slipping out of the room with a wink, hiding herself behind the drapes in the hall so that she could watch out for Grey's reappearance.

"Well?" Blaise turned to Sara in impatience. "Why are you doing this?"

She looked at him quickly, hearing the anger in his voice. "Doing what? I don't understand."

"You understand very well." He had no time for courtesy, for Grey would be back at any moment. "Why did you agree to marry your cousin?"

"I . . . I . . . cannot see how that can concern you."

She tried to put a bold front on it, but he swore under his breath.

"It does concern me, and if you are telling me politely to mind my own business, I would remind you that you gave me the right to ask such questions when you came to me for help."

She flinched. "Yes, I know. It was wrong of me to come; wrong of me to bother you."

"I didn't think so at the time; I don't think so now. Tell me the truth; why are you marrying Sidney?"

"Uncle Arthur thinks it is best."

"But why?"

"I . . . can't explain. It is too difficult for me to . . . to . . . make you understand."

"I am not simple. I am quite quick to grasp the essentials of a situation."

"You are angry."

He met her sad eyes with a feeling of helpless frustration. She had stopped fighting. Whatever it was that was frightening and tormenting her, she had now given in to it.

"Do you wonder? I am entitled to be angry since you will not tell me what is wrong, and why you are doing this thing. Sara, you know you cannot marry this boy."

"I must." She rose, trying to move away from him because to be near to him was too dangerous and too painful. "You don't understand; I must marry him."

He caught her by the arms and pulled her close to him, seeing the smudges under her eyes, the cheekbones sharper because she had grown so thin.

"If I don't understand, then make it clear to me. Hurry, Sara, there isn't much time. Grey will be back in a moment, and God knows how I can get to see you alone again. Tell me; what is it?"

She opened her mouth, feeling the strength of his hands give her new hope and courage.

"Well, you see...."

It was all she had time to say, for Laura was back in the room warning them that Grey was approaching. Blaise swore aloud, and Sara sat down again, feeling the brief hope drain out of her.

When Westerbrook had gone, Sara went back to her room, collecting her letters from the hall as she went.

There was yet another letter, and she gave a small cry of disgust. This time she wouldn't open it; this time she would destroy it before it could defile her again, but her good intentions did not last, and soon she was reading it, beaten and cringing beneath the dreadful words.

She almost ran to the window, anxious to get a glimpse of the square where normal people were going about their business, but as she looked down she saw the old woman again, staring up at the window.

Sara felt as though she were drunk, reeling as she got to the bed and lying on it face downwards. It seemed to her that the whole world was growing dark, and that she was surrounded by malice and hatred and perhaps something more awful still. She thought of Blaise Westerbrook, but that made it worse. He had held her tightly; so tightly that she could still feel the pressure of his fingers on her arms. He had been so close that she could have lifted her head and touched his mouth with her own, if she had dared, but she had not dared. She had agreed to marry Sidney; it was like a sentence of death.

She got up quickly. It was impossible to be alone any longer if she were to hold on to her reason, and she hurried downstairs, stopping abruptly as she saw Arthur Grey in the hall. He was shewing a shabbily-dressed man to the front door, and for a moment her brows met in a frown. The visitor was not the normal kind of caller, and it was unusual for Grey not to have summoned Laura or Maud to shew him out. Then she dismissed the matter; it was of no importance.

In the sitting-room that afternoon Rachel was listing last-minute guests who would have to be invited to the wedding.

Henrietta was pouring the tea.

"Did we ask the Pearsons?"

"Yes, mama, they are coming."

"Is Matthew coming?" Rebecca said it innocently, addressing herself to Mercy Thorne who had picked up her sewing basket. "Is he, Mercy?"

Mercy's sallow face flushed, and Rachel said firmly:

"No, Rebecca, he is not. He is not family."

"Neither are the Pearsons or most of the other guests; they are just friends. And you are mistaken, mama. Matthew is a relation, isn't he?"

"Not of mine."

"I want him to come."

"Rebecca, if you cannot be quiet, go to your room. I must finish this list and your incessant talking is quite distracting me."

Rachel looked up as Grey came into the room surprised to

find him home at that hour of the day.

"Arthur? I had not thought to see you until six o'clock. Is something wrong?"

"It is Sidney, my dear."

"Sidney?" Rachel was blank. "What about Sidney?"

Sara felt a new flutter of alarm as Grey hesitated.

"He was attacked last night."

"What! Arthur, what are you saying? How could he have been attacked? He is staying with the Rossmans."

"Yes, yes, I know." Grey was almost testy. "I am aware of that. Sidney and the Rossman boys went out last night, to a music hall I believe. On the way home it grew foggy. Somehow Sidney got separated from Basil and George. They thought they heard someone cry out but they weren't sure and so they went on, but when they got to Chantry Street and found that there was no sign of Sidney, they retraced their steps."

"But is he hurt? What happened?"

Everyone was staring at Grey, willing him to go on.

"He had been jumped on and knocked unconscious. He's not hurt, Rachel; no need to worry. It was a bump on the head, nothing more."

"But who would do such a thing?"

"There are plenty of thieves about and the fog gives them cover."

Grey glanced at Henrietta.

"That's the odd thing. Nothing was taken. He still had his watch and his wallet when Basil and George found him."

"Then who...."

"I doubt that we'll ever know now." Grey took his tea and sat down. 'Sidney doesn't remember anything apparently, just that someone hit him from behind. It's a rum business, but thank God he's come to no harm."

"Perhaps someone didn't want him to marry Sara."

Rebecca said it dreamily, waiting for the storm to break about her unrepentant head.

"Rebecca, what have I told you? Arthur, you must speak

to this girl; she is in a most rebellious mood today. I was about to send her to her room when you came in."

Grey looked at Rebecca thoughtfully. "You mustn't upset your mother, you know, I won't have that. Why should anyone want to stop Sidney from marrying Sara? It's a queer thing to say."

Rebecca pouted. She wasn't used to being reprimanded by her father, particularly in front of the others.

"Well, if there was someone else who wanted to marry her, he might be glad to see Sidney out of the way."

"That is nonsense," snapped Rachel crossly. "You'll upset Sara if you go on like this, and we don't want her to be more. . . ." She broke off abruptly. "Be quiet, Rebecca, you've said quite enough."

"But who does want to marry Sara, other than Sidney?" Grey was tugging at his beard, watching Rebecca almost broodingly. "Aren't you being fanciful, m'dear?"

"No I'm not." Rebecca tossed her head. "Matthew Compton wanted to marry her, I'm sure of it."

"Rebecca!"

"How can you be so wicked as to accuse Matthew?"

"Really, Rebecca!"

Rebecca grew sullen as Rachel, Mercy and Henrietta vented their vexation upon her. Sara grew colder still. How had Rebecca known that Matthew had spoken of marriage? She must have been listening at the key-hole, or someone else had done so and faithfully reported the result to Rebecca. No wonder Rebecca hated her.

Grey put down his cup and said firmly:

"I will not ask you how you know this, Rebecca, and I hope that you have no cause to be ashamed on that score, but are you certain young Compton wanted to marry Sara?"

"Yes I am." Rebecca was defiant. "Mercy knows I'm telling the truth, don't you, Mercy? You know how Matthew feels about Sara."

"I know no such thing." Mercy did not look up from her

mending. "I think you are making the whole thing up, and if I had been so wicked when I was your age, my father would have taken a stick to me."

"And that is what your father should do to you," said Rachel angrily. "Now go to your room and stay there. Maud shall bring you a tray later on. We do not want to see you downstairs again to-day."

Rebecca flounced out of the room and Sara turned to ask Grey whether Sidney was really unharmed, but the words died on her lips.

Grey was looking at Mercy Thorne in the strangest way, with something in his eyes which Sara had never seen before. Then he glanced away and gave Sara a quick smile.

"Take no notice of Rebecca," he said softly. "She means no real harm. It's just a bit of jealousy, nothing more. Forget it now and get me another cup of tea, there's a good girl. It's been a difficult day."

The fog came down again the next night. Matthew Compton left the pub on the corner of Grantbridge Road and began to feel his way towards his lodgings. He had had a good meal and a pint or two of strong beer, and the fog wasn't really bothering him. He was used to it, like all Londoners, and his journey wasn't a long one; just across the road and along the park railings and he'd be home.

He had been walking for about three minutes when he heard the footsteps behind him. At first he took no notice, for there was nothing out of the way in finding someone else making tracks for home. But after he had paused once or twice, making sure that he was not losing his way, he noticed that the footsteps stopped too, and he glanced over his shoulder, trying to catch a glimpse of the person behind him.

There was no one to be seen. He shrugged. It was his imagination, or the beer. On a night like this it was easy to let one's mind play tricks on one.

He kept close to the railings, glad of their support, but then he heard the footsteps again. There was no mistaking it; someone was following him.

He told himself he was being a fool. Why shouldn't there be someone else taking the same route as he? It was ludicrous to suppose that there was anything sinister in the measured tread behind him. Nevertheless, he tried to quicken his own step, acutely aware that the sound behind him was growing louder.

Finally he turned round and shouted out:

"Who's there? Do you hear me? What do you want?"

His voice echoed back at him, rebounding against the impenetrable blanket of fog.

"Who is it? Do you hear what I say? What do you want?"

It was very quiet and still. Matthew felt as if he were completely alone in the world, for now he could neither hear anything nor see beyond his outstretched hand. Frantic he spun round again and tried to run.

When he felt the thing go round his throat, he got out one hoarse scream, struggling madly to loosen the cord which was tightening with every second and making his eyes start out of his head. He could feel the whole universe rocking about him, and there were drums beating furiously in his temples, his breath dying in a gasp as the final jerk ended his life.

When the police called at Candle Square to tell Mercy Thorne what had happened, she fainted in an untidy heap on the hall floor. Laura and Maud cried out in fright, and Henrietta, who had heard the commotion, hurried up with smelling salts and a damp cloth for Mercy's forehead.

When they had got her into the sitting-room, they gave her a tot of brandy, waiting until she opened her eyes.

Later that evening the family tried to comfort her, but she did not respond. She knew that they had all disliked Matthew in varying degrees, and that not one of them was in the least sorry that he was dead.

"It is odd that Matthew should have been attacked like Sidney." Rebecca had been crying, but was forcing herself to be calm. "Do you think it was the same person?"

"Of course not." Henrietta was irritable. She was concerned by Mercy's appearance and even more so by what was happening. Rebecca was right; it was rather extraordinary, yet her sister must not be allowed to make a drama out of it. "It was obviously a different man. I understand Matthew's money was stolen."

"And his watch, the one I gave him." Mercy said drearily. "I don't know how I shall break the news to my sister."

"Shall I do it for you?" asked Henrietta quickly. "I know it must be painful for you, Mercy. Let me do it."

"No, no, I'll do it myself later on."

"A terrible thing; quite terrible." Grey patted Mercy on the shoulder. "I know how you felt about him, m'dear. A dreadful thing."

"Do you, Arthur?" Mercy's red-rimmed eyes met his. "I doubt if anyone knows what I felt for Matthew. He was like my own. I couldn't have loved him more if he'd been my son."

"Quite so, quite so."

"Well now he's gone." Mercy got up and straightened her dress. "No need for you to worry about him coming here again, Rachel. He's dead now."

"Well really!"

Rachel watched Mercy close the door behind her, indignant as she denied any responsibility for Matthew's lack of welcome.

"Sometimes I think Mercy goes out of her way to be unpleasant. We let the boy come here, didn't we? You did not forbid him to come, did you, Arthur?"

"No, Rachel, I didn't." He forbore to remind her that she had instructed him to do so. "It seemed harsh to do so, and after all he was Mercy's nephew. And now, my dear, I have to go out."

"Again? It is late, Arthur, can't it wait until morning, whatever it is?"

"I'm afraid not. It is a matter of business and that, like time and tide, waits for no man. I won't disturb you when I come in; I'll sleep in the dressing-room."

He left the room before Rachel could start to protest again, humming to himself as he made his way down the front steps and hailed a passing hansom.

"That's a lot of money, m'dear."

Grey was lying on Candace's bed waiting for her to undress. He always like to watch her disrobe, for her every movement was graceful and it excited him to see the whiteness of her flesh appear bit by bit.

"My bills are heavy, and a thousand pounds is nothing to a man as rich as you."

Candace watched Grey's face in the mirror, laughing inwardly at his expression, but there was no real humour in her. She felt quite cold-blooded about Grey, and was prepared to make him pay for the privileges he sought so eagerly. She unfastened her long auburn hair, laying the pins down carefully in a small crystal tray.

"What can you have bought which cost so much?"

Candace let the robe slip an inch or two, still watching his reflection.

"Oh, I can't remember exactly. Boots, furs, some new gowns; a hat or two."

"Those couldn't have cost so much."

"Well, there were other things too. Am I becoming too expensive for you?"

She turned from the mirror, letting the garment fall away, standing naked before him. She saw his face suffuse with colour and felt the scorn tremble on her tongue. She wanted to shout at him and tell him how stupid he looked with desire glazing his eyes and his mouth loose and half-open.

"No, no, of course not," he said thickly, reaching out for her, but she moved away, just out of range of his hand. "Come here; don't go."

She came forward again, letting him feast his eyes on the motion of her body, seeing the saliva at the corner of his mouth.

"How can I relax when I am so worried about money?" She pouted gently. "How can I make you happy, if I am not happy myself?"

"I'll give it to you; whatever you want." Grey caught her arm and pulled her on to the bed. "For Christ's sake come here, girl. Don't you know what you're doing to me?"

She let him make love to her, throwing herself wholeheartedly into the job, for she never cheated a man who was prepared to pay; thinking of Blaise whilst Grey's sweaty hands fumbled over her. When he was finally sated, lying back in a state of near exhaustion, she said casually :

"You won't forget your promise, will you?"

He shook his head. "No, you'll have your money. I'll bring it to-morrow night."

"Not to-morrow." She put on her robe, tying it about her slender waist. "The night after."

"I suppose you've got someone else coming to-morrow."

She gave a gurgle of laughter.

"Come, Mr. Brown, I'm your mistress, not your wife."

"I wish you were my wife."

"You couldn't afford me."

"Yes I could." Grey sat up and swung his legs to the floor. "I've enough money to keep you in whatever style you choose."

"Have you?" She was mocking him now, wishing he would go so that she could get some sleep. "I would want diamonds, you know."

"I've given you some."

"Only small ones. I would want necklaces, rings and bracelets, and...."

"You don't care a damn about me, do you?"

She gave him an ironic look. "I let you make love to me."

"That's not the same thing. I pay for that."

"You're not very chivalrous."

"No, just honest. I wish you were honest with me."

"I am." She sat on the edge of the bed and watched him

dress. "I've never lied to you, Mr. Brown. I've never pretended that you were the only one."

"No, you've never done that," he agreed, and fastened his waistcoat. "You'll let me come again?"

"Of course, why not? You're going to bring me a present, aren't you?"

"I meant after that."

"Certainly, provided you can pay."

"You're damned cruel, Candace."

"And you're becoming sentimental. Be content with what you have. You want my body; I'm prepared to sell it to you now and then."

"How can you talk like that?"

"Because it is true. You say you want me to be honest, so I am. Now you must go. I shall look old if I don't get my sleep."

"You'll never do that. Here, give me another kiss."

Candace let him hold her for a moment, enduring his embrace until he released her with a shuddering sigh.

"Night after to-morrow, eh?"

She smiled slowly and patted his cheek.

'That's right, and don't forget my present. Goodbye, Mr. Brown."

The next evening Candace was in a very different mood. She felt calm and contented as she sat in her bedroom waiting for Blaise Westerbrook. The news that the girl in Candle Square was going to marry her cousin had lifted a heavy weight from her heart, and although she still had doubts about Blaise's intentions towards herself, at least there was no serious rival on the horizon for the time being.

There were other matters, of a more mundane and practical character, which pleased her too. Arthur Grey was not the only one of her clients who had been persuaded to part with large sums of money, and now she had a comfortable balance in the bank and no outstanding debts to pay. She paused to think about Grey for a moment. He was the most ardent of them all, almost embarrassingly so at times. Most of her visitors were satisfied with a relationship kept on a light and purely physical basis, but Grey was clearly in love. She knew she should have been flattered, but she wasn't. It became a pleasure to deny him now and then, watching his misery as she rejected him.

Naturally the rejection was not too final, for Grey made handsome gifts. Candace looked round the room and a faint smile touched her lips. The austerity of the schoolgirl's boudoir had gone, for that very morning the new red velvet curtains had been hung, the sprawling sheepskin rugs laid on the floor. Candace had spent extravagantly on ornate mirrors for the walls, silver and porcelain fitments for the dressing-table and armchairs with white satin covers.

Blaise arrived at ten, raising his eyebrows as he touched her cheek absentmindedly with his lips.

"Good God, Candace, what have you done? It looks like a whore-house."

Her nostrils grew pinched with vexation, but she did not spit out at him as she would have done a week or two ago. There was too much at stake now, and her tone had only a hint of acid in it as she replied.

"Well, sweet, it is a whore-house, isn't it?"

"Maybe, but it wasn't so obvious before. What made you change it?"

"I was tired of it as it was. It was dull."

"But in passably good taste."

"And this is not?"

He looked down at her, hearing her irritation.

"You know damned well it isn't."

"I like it, and you don't have to look at it."

"That's true. I can look at you instead." He raised her chin with his hand, studying the slanting green eyes smouldering with anger, and the wide beautiful mouth. "You at least have not changed beyond recognition."

"I'm glad."

She would have pulled away from him, but he held her firmly by the arm, grinning at her as she bit her lip.

"No tantrums to-night, Candace. That is not what I've come for."

"Why did you come?"

"To sleep with you, what else?"

He pulled her wrap off her shoulders and bent his head to kiss her.

"Where did you get this rag?"

"You don't like that either, I presume?"

"No, I don't, but I like what is beneath it. Stop talking, girl, and come to bed."

Candace's temper was soon gone, for Blaise Westerbrook could drive everything out of her mind when he made love to her. It was like a tempest rushing through her, cleansing her brain and soul with its completeness. She wanted the moment of fulfilment to last for ever, but of course it never did, and soon Blaise was propping himself up against the pillows and lighting a cigar. They talked for a while, no longer gibing at each other. Candace thought how restful and intimate it was simply to lie there next to him, discussing anything and everything, as a husband and wife might do.

When Blaise had dressed, she rose reluctantly, throwing aside her offending robe of transparent red silk.

"Dearest, get me another wrap from the cupboard." She sat at the dressing-table and began to smooth her rumpled hair. "The green satin is there; you like that, don't you?"

"It is as good as anything, if you must dress."

She gave a low laugh. "I will stay naked, if it will please you."

"It would, but you might catch cold, and I have to go before long."

He opened the cupboard, finding the green peignoir without difficulty, and was about to close the door again when he glanced down, his hand frozen in mid-air. He looked quickly over his shoulder, but Candace had gone into the adjoining bathroom, and he stooped to pull at the object which had caught his attention. It was in a box, only an inch or two of it showing, clearly intended to be hidden from prying eyes. He picked it up and stared at it for a long time, a hundred unanswered questions churning about in his brain as he tried to make sense of what he was looking at.

Then he heard Candace shut the bathroom door and in a second he had returned the object to its box and closed the closet door.

"Do you have to go so soon, Blaise?"

Westerbrook helped Candace into her wrap, keeping his face blank and his voice flat. He was not ready to question Candace yet; that would have to be done later.

"I'm afraid so."

"When will you come again?"

"Soon."

"You promise?"

She was looking up at him, pleading with her eyes for an assurance, and he nodded slowly, not responding to the touch of her hand on his.

"Oh yes I promise, Candace. You may rest assured; I shall be back before long."

Two days before the wedding, Henrietta went to Sara's room. She crossed to the chest of drawers and laid a pile of clean underclothes on the top of it.

"I've brought these up for you," she said, smoothing the petticoats with nervous fingers. "I thought it would save Maud a journey."

"Thank you." Sara waited. It was clear that Henrietta had something else to say, for she made no attempt to move. "It was kind of you, Henrietta."

"Sara." Henrietta was finding it difficult to begin, but it was obvious that what she had to say was important. "Sara, you and I have not been very close. It is not that I'm not fond of you, but somehow I find it difficult to . . . to . . . shew other people what I feel. Do you understand?"

"I think so."

Sara was puzzled, but she did not want to drive her cousin away by saying too much.

"And lately, of course, I have had to spend so much time with mama that there hasn't been the opportunity to . . . well . . . to be with others."

"No, of course not."

There was an uncomfortable pause. Then Henrietta said rapidly:

"Sara, you shouldn't marry Sidney. I know that the wedding is in two days, but there is still time to stop it. Tell papa that you have changed your mind."

Sara could feel her pulse racing, but she tried to be calm.

"But why? Don't you feel that I am good enough for Sidney? Is it because you think that I may not be . . . well . . . quite. . . ."

"No, no, it is nothing to do with that." Henrietta's normally blank face was working with some strong emotion, her eyes moist with tears. "No, Sara, it is nothing to do with you. It is just that. . . ."

"Just what? Henrietta, what are you trying to say?"

"It is difficult to explain. It's just that I know it is wrong for you to marry Sidney. You mustn't marry him! If you can't bring yourself to tell papa and face the consequences, run away. Go anywhere, but don't marry my brother."

Sara looked into Henrietta's eyes and saw something awful there. She wasn't sure what it was, and the look was gone in an instant, but it was something never to be forgotten.

Her lips felt stiff as she said quietly:

"I can't run away."

"And you won't tell father that the wedding cannot take place?"

"I can't do that either."

Henrietta's face closed up again, mask-like as she nodded

in acceptance of defeat.

"Very well, but I have tried to warn you. Remember that, Sara, if . . . when things go wrong. I did try to warn you."

She went out quietly, leaving Sara staring after her. Then Sara got up and went to the window. It was all very normal that morning; no old woman, no anonymous letters. Her hand was gripping the curtain, screwing it up as a new thought struck her. Was Henrietta sending the letters? Beyond doubt she had been in deadly earnest when she had tried to stop the marriage. Had she tried to stop it earlier by other methods and, when these had failed, come out into the open in a last attempt? Was she jealous because it was now obvious that she would never marry? It was known that spinsters sometimes turned sour and hit out spitefully in secretive ways against those more favoured than themselves.

And that momentary look in Henrietta's eyes; that had been terrible. Sara shuddered. She closed her eyes for a second. Whatever it was, Henrietta wouldn't come again and she, Sara, would never know what was wrong until it was too late.

NINE

Sara's wedding day dawned bright and clear, frosty, with a weak sun to cheer the desolation of mid-January.

The household was up earlier than usual, Maud and Laura beginning their tasks at five-thirty, for every inch of the house had to be cleaned and dusted ready for the reception and wedding breakfast. Sara had coffee in her room, but that was her last moment of solitude, for then she was whisked off to Henrietta's room where a hip bath had been filled in front of the fire, and where all the wedding finery was laid out in spectacular array.

Sara felt no emotion at all. She was not even nervous as Maud and Laura helped her to bath and don her undergarments, before stepping back to allow Mercy and Henrietta to attend to the dress itself. She could not really believe that the day had finally come.

"It's a beautiful frock," Mercy said grudgingly. "You look very well, Sara, but you're too pale."

"All brides are pale." Aunt Rachel had come to watch the final proceedings. "I was as white as whey on my wedding day. Yes, you look handsome enough, Sara. Turn round and let me see the back."

Finally everyone was ready.

"This is a happy moment for me," Arthur whispered to Sara as they left the house together, pausing on the steps as the coachman opened the door of the carriage. "You will never know what this day means to me, my dear. Come now, we have kept Sidney waiting long enough."

But Sidney was not waiting. An agitated usher rushed up

to the brougham to inform Grey that the bride would have to take another turn round the houses, for the groom was not yet in sight. Grey frowned, but at first he was not unduly worried.

"What a thing!" He was jovial as he bade the coachman set off again. "I'll have something to say to the boy when I see him. Never mind, m'dear, I expect something's delayed him. We'll take another turn round the block and he'll be there by the time we get back."

But he wasn't, and an hour later there was still no sign of Sidney Grey. By now the church was abuzz with whispers and speculation, and Rachel was in tears, threatening to go home. Grey comforted her, bidding her to wait a while longer, perspiration standing out on his forehead as he made excuses to the restive wedding guests who were growing tired of waiting.

Half an hour later, even Arthur Grey had to admit that his son was not coming. He made the announcement in a voice which shook, excusing the inexcusable with a hint of illness. No one believed him, and they filed out of the church indignantly, making no secret of what they thought about a man who jilted his bride at the altar.

Sara was numb. She let Laura and Maud help her off with the frothy dress, watching them hang it up with a quick twitter of shocked exictement. Henrietta brought her a warm dressing-gown to slip on, and Mercy produced piping-hot coffee.

They stayed with Sara until Arthur Grey returned from Chelsea, eyeing him expectantly as he sank into a chair and wiped his brow.

"Well?" Rachel's eyes were red from weeping. She had never been so mortified in all her life. "Where is he? Arthur, did you tell him. . . ?"

"He wasn't there."

Sara turned her head to glance at Arthur. He looked as though the breath had been knocked out of him; old and crumpled in the harsh light of the winter's afternoon.

"What do you mean, he wasn't there?"

"What I say, Rachel; he wasn't there."

"Then where is he?"

"No one knows. Just as Sidney and Basil Rossman were setting off, Basil realised that he had forgotten the ring. He told Sidney to go on in case the delay made him late. He saw the coach go off with Sidney in it."

Rachel's mouth opened like a fish gasping for water.

"Well? If he set off, why didn't he arrive at the church?"

"I don't know. No one does."

"But that is ridiculous. Arthur, you must do something. Doesn't Sidney realise what he has done? Doesn't he know that he has made fools of all of us? And what about Sara? Does he understand what he has done to her?"

"I have no idea," Grey said wearily, as if it were an effort to speak. "How can I know, since he isn't here to ask? As to why he didn't arrive . . . well . . . I can't answer that either."

"Have you been to the police? Perhaps there was an accident."

Grey nodded to Henrietta whose own face was like bleached calico.

"Yes, I've seen the police. No accident reported so far. They're looking into it."

Rachel began to cry again. "How can he have vanished without trace? Someone must have seen him."

"Don't upset yourself, mama." Henrietta laid a soothing hand on Rachel's shoulder. "You will make yourself ill. Come, I'll take you back to your room and you can rest."

"Oh, Henrietta, what am I going to do?"

Henrietta and Mercy led the wailing Rachel away, and Grey said slowly:

"What are any of us going to do?"

"I'm sorry, uncle."

He looked up at Sara and tried to smile.

"I know you are, m'dear. Worse for you than for anyone, of course. I don't understand it; I just don't understand it."

"Perhaps the police will find out something."

"I hope so, though how they'll do it I can't imagine."

And when the police did call it was to offer very poor comfort. Grey spent half an hour with them in his study and then returned to the drawing-room where the family had assembled, waiting for news.

"They haven't found him, or anyone who's seen him. They're as mystified as we are, except that...."

"What, papa?"

"They think he went of his own free will."

"Father!"

He closed his eyes, leaning forward so that they should not see the moisture on his cheeks.

"I know it isn't true. Sidney wouldn't do such a thing, but that's what they think. They say it does happen sometimes. Men lose their nerve and can't go through with it. You see, they can't find the carriage or the coachman either. They think Sidney paid the man to drive him somewhere."

"Perhaps Sidney did run away." Rebecca's voice was taut as she turned to glare at Sara. "Perhaps he couldn't face marrying Sara, and who could bl..."

"Be quiet, Rebecca." Henrietta snapped the words off, moving to rest her hand on Grey's arm. "Father, I'm sure Sidney wouldn't do that."

"So am I, but I couldn't make them believe it. They said they'd go on making enquiries, of course, but I doubt that there's much they can do."

"But someone must do something." Henrietta bit her lip. "We can't just pretend it hasn't happened. Sidney has disappeared. We've got to try to find him."

"We will, we will." Grey was pulling himself together with an effort. "There are such things as private agencies you know. I'll get in touch with one to-morrow. Nothing more we can do for the moment but pray. After dinner, I'll go and see the Rossmans again. Perhaps Basil will have remembered something by now which might help."

When Grey had been to Chelsea, finding nothing new to assist him in solving the riddle of Sidney's disappearance, he went on to St. John's Wood to see Candace.

"I didn't expect to see you to-night, Mr. Brown. You're lucky to find me in."

"I didn't expect to come to-night. It was to have been my son's wedding day."

"Was to have been?"

She looked at him quickly, seeing the ashy quality of his face.

He told her what had happened whilst she poured him some whisky which he downed in a single gulp.

"I'm sorry." She hesitated, not quite sure what to say. "Can I do anything?"

He shook his head. "To-morrow I'll get a man on to it, though God knows if he'll find anything."

"Could the police be right? It's the only rational explanation."

"That Sidney couldn't face marriage? I won't believe it."

"You don't want to believe it."

"Perhaps not."

"If it were true, would he get in touch with you, do you think?"

Grey shrugged. "Who knows? Depends why he ran away, if he did. I don't think he did."

"Something will turn up." She gave him back his refilled glass. "Don't think about it for a while. Sometimes it's good to get away from things which make you unhappy."

He seemed to see her for the first time, catching her hand and resting his lips against it.

"I know, that's why I came. I needed you to-night."

"No, not to-night," she said firmly, trying to draw away from him. "I told you, I hadn't expected you."

"Does it matter?" He wouldn't let her go, pulling her nearer to him. "I really need you, Candace, especially to-night. Don't send me away. Let me be with you."

"What about your wife? Won't she expect you to be home?"

"I'll go home later on. She thinks I'm in Chelsea. She won't miss me yet. Please, Candace."

She forced herself to be brutal in an effort to get rid of him.

"My comfort is expensive, you know that."

He looked at her as though she had kicked him, and she felt curiously triumphant. The twinge of sympathy she had had for him when she heard his news was gone and it was no effort now to be savage.

"I know." He tried to make a joke of it and failed miserably. "You'll make a bankrupt of me."

"I've no use for bankrupts."

He winced and said hurriedly:

"I didn't mean it. I'll give you more money if you want it; that is no problem. I'm not a poor man, and besides I'm expecting an investment to pay off handsomely in the near future. But now, Candace...."

"I want to change the furnishings downstairs." She began to take off her dress, slowly and deliberately. "I've done this room, as you can see, but the drawing-room bores me. I want it blue and gold."

"Will it cost a lot?"

"A small fortune I should think. Is it too rich for your blood, Mr. Brown?"

"No." His voice was hoarse, and he was starting to take off his coat. "Christ, you're beautiful."

"So men tell me." She wasn't ready to give in to him yet. "There is one who would like me to become his alone. He wants me to send the rest of you packing."

"You won't?" He was almost panic-stricken, fumbling with his trousers. "Candace, you wouldn't! I couldn't live without you. Life would be nothing unless I could come here now and then and be with you."

"I haven't made up my mind yet." She turned the screw, letting the chemise flutter to the ground, pulling the petticoats off so that they fell in a froth of lawn at her feet. "Maybe I will, maybe I won't."

She finished removing her stockings, running a hand up her thigh as if the feel of the creamy skin pleased her.

"Well, Mr. Brown?"

He flung the last garment away from him, kneeling at her feet and clasping her body to him. She could feel his tears against her flesh, her mouth moving in scorn.

Marie-Amélia was right. How could one have affection for a door-mat?

"And so you think, my lord, you may have found the answer?"

Augustine Dean helped Westerbrook into his evening jacket.

"Not all the answers." Blaise's face was very still. "What I think I have discovered could not be the solution to everything, but it is the first chink of light which I have seen. The first key to the first lock."

Dean gave a small smile.

"Arnold Roper was full of the latest scandal from Candle Square when he called to-day. The missing bridegroom, of course."

"Of course." Westerbrook's well-shaped mouth moved in a humourless grimace. "That at least is a blessing. Sara is spared matrimony for the time being. What do the servants imagine happened to Sidney?"

"They favour the police's theory. They think Master Sidney got cold feet and ran away, paying the coachman to keep out of the way so that no one could question him."

"Does Roper know what Sara thinks?"

"He didn't say, my lord. Maud says she spends most of her time in her room."

"Yes, I see. They do not think she is in any way responsible for Sidney's disappearance?"

"No, except that he was running away from her. They still believe her funny in the head, of course, especially since Christmas when Miss Sara claimed she saw a face at the window which wasn't human."

"Mm. No one else saw that, of course."

"No one."

"Doubtless no one else was meant to see it."

"My lord?"

"Nothing, I was thinking aloud. Augustine, to-morrow we must begin more investigations. There are people we must find and talk to if we are to get all the answers we need. I have made a list; it is on the desk in my study. Give it to Roper and tell him to do what he can, and quickly. I've made some notes about things which might be useful to him. Tell him to take on more help if he needs it. I sense that time is running out for us."

"Yes, my lord. Will you be back to-night?"

"I'm not sure." Blaise adjusted the fold of his evening cloak and smiled unpleasantly. "It depends how rusty the key is in the lock and how long it takes me to turn it. Don't wait up."

Westerbrook got to St. John's Wood at midnight. Bessie Poke's face reflected her consternation as she opened the door, but her hurried explanation that Candace was out availed her nothing. Blaise pushed past her and slammed the door behind him.

"She is in," he said baldly. "The lights are on in her bedroom."

"I was up there, not a minute ago, turnin' the bed down."

"They've been on half an hour or more. Besides, I saw her visitor arrive."

Bessie's plump face was flushed. "She weren't expectin' you."

"I am aware of that, and I will not embarrass her by bursting into her bedroom whilst she is entertaining her guest. Let us go into the kitchen and wait for her."

Bessie had no chance to protest, for Blaise was bundling her unceremoniously through the door at the end of the passage. He looked around the kitchen with approval, for it was as spotless as the rest of the house and very homely after

Candace's lush boudoir.

"Very nice, Bessie. You are a good housekeeper."

"I do me best, sir, but...."

"You do lots of things for Miss Martin, don't you?"

"Things?" She looked vacant. "You mean cookin' and such?"

"Those, certainly, but your talents do not end with mere domestic chores, do they?"

"I don't know what you mean, sir. Will you 'ave a cup of tea?"

"Thank you, no. And you do know what I mean, Bessie. You're not stupid."

"Maybe not, but I...."

Bessie was saved the labour of wriggling out of Westerbrook's interrogation by the sound of the front door closing. Blaise gave the maid a caustic smile.

"My turn now, Bessie. You'll stay in this room if you know what's good for you. Whatever you may hear, don't interfere."

Blaise took the stairs three at a time, striding into the bedroom without knocking.

"Is that you, Bessie?" Candace called out from the bathroom. "He's gone, thank God. Get me a gin, will you?"

Blaise closed the door and went to the side table under the window where Candace kept a few bottles of spirits. He poured a large measure of gin into a glass and went into the bathroom.

For a moment he stood in the doorway, looking down at Candace in the bath, her body half-submerged in the scented water, her eyes closed.

"You find that refreshing, do you? Or are you washing your sins away?"

Candace opened her eyes and sat up abruptly, holding a large sponge against her. He gave a bleak laugh.

"A trifle late for modesty, don't you think? There is no part of your body with which I am not entirely familiar. Here is your gin."

"What are you doing here, Blaise? You said you would not come until Thursday."

"I changed my mind. Do you want this drink or not?"

She took it and swallowed it hastily.

"Give me a towel, dearest, will you? That one, on the stool."

He threw it at her, not caring that it nearly knocked the glass out of her hand.

"Get out of there, Candace, I want to talk to you."

"But...."

"Do as I tell you and be quick about it. I haven't got all night to waste.

He went back to the bedroom and waited for her, pouring himself a brandy and surveying Candace's new furnishings with a sardonic eye. When she joined him, she was off-balance and rather angry.

"What is wrong with you, Blaise?" She sat down in front of the mirror and began to brush her hair. "You're in a vile mood to-night. Why did you come?"

"To ask you some questions."

"What kind of questions? Can't they wait until to-morrow; I'm tired."

You should pursue a more restful occupation." He came to stand behind her, watching her in the glass. "Was he very exhausting, my dear Candace?"

She reddened. Blaise knew, of course, that other men visited her, but hitherto she had been able to avoid throwing the fact in his face. But it was his own fault, and she said so roundly.

"I've never pretended with you. If I'd known you were coming, I would have put him off."

"And had him pine away for lack of your loving? That would have been too cruel, but then you are cruel, aren't you? I've only just realised it."

She laid down the brush, meeting his eyes squarely.

"I don't know what you are talking about. If you thought me cruel because I let other men come here, you had only to say so. If I had known that you wanted another kind of arrangement with me, I would have been delighted, you know that."

"Another kind of arrangement?" He frowned. "What do you mean?"

"I would have been your mistress only, had you wished it. Or, if you had wanted something more...." Her voice softened. "If you had wanted something more permanent, my love, no one would have been happier than I."

"Permanent?" The frown was deeper. "What are you talking about?"

She took her courage in both hands. It was now or never.

"I'm talking about marriage."

He stared at her for a long moment, then he threw back his head and laughed. It was an ugly sound, jarring on her nerves and making her shrink inside herself.

"God Almighty, are you serious?" He stopped laughing and his face had grown as cold as stone. "Do you honestly expect me to believe that you thought I would marry a jade like you?"

She whitened under the verbal lash.

"Why not? It has been done before."

"But not by me. Do you think I want a harlot to bear my sons for me?"

She was chilled to the bone, despite the warmth of the room. She had failed and she knew it. She could see the pieces of her ambitions lying round her in fragments. Only one thing had to be salvaged; her pride.

She picked up a comb and ran it through her hair, shrugging as if his words were of no significance.

"Please yourself. Marry some dull little frump if you want to. It's all one to me."

"Not all decent women are frumps, you know, but this is not what I came to discuss."

"No?" She was indifferent. "I'm at a loss to know why you did come, since you've been bad-tempered and rude ever since you arrived. If you want to come to bed, so well and good. If you don't, go away, so that I can finish undressing."

"You are already undressed. It is an habitual state with you. I want to talk to you about Candle Square, and what you keep in the bottom of that cupboard over there."

He saw her face drain of colour and smiled savagely.

"Yes, by dear Candace, I want to talk of Candle Square. You know quite a lot about No: 11 and its inhabitants, don't you?"

"I've no idea what you mean. Where is Candle Square, for heaven's sake?"

"In Kensington, but you already know that. Don't lie to me, or I'll make you sorry you were born."

"I know nothing about it. Do go away, Blaise."

She tried to get up but he thrust her down with a violent hand.

"Stay where you are. We have hardly begun this conversation yet, for we've wasted so much time talking about your fantasies. Now, how did you get to know Sara Lessingham? Who told you her name and where she lived?"

"Who?"

"I shall not ask you again."

"I have told you, I don't know . . . ah!"

She cried out as he spun her round and struck her across the face.

"I warned you. Now, how did you find out about her?"

"I don't know anyone called Lessingham. Blaise, really you. . . ."

When he hit her again she gave a small sob, slipping from the stool and trying to reach the bed. He caught her half-way across the floor and threw her roughly on to the crimson and gold coverlet.

"And who else do you know who lives there? There has to be someone. Who is it?"

"Blaise, please!"

He bared his teeth and went to the cupboard, opening the

door and bending down to reach into the box he had found before. When he came back he had something in his hand which made Candace cry out, and he nodded, his eyes like ice.

"Yes, Candace, yes. You see I discovered this last time I called, but I wasn't ready to question you then. Now I am, and before I go you will answer each and everyone of those questions or I will beat you senseless. Do you understand me?"

She did not reply, lying dumb and terrified. She watched his face, growing cold inside.

"I will ask you just once more, Candace," he said very softly. "Just once more."

When he had gone, Candace rolled off the bed and dragged herself into the bathroom. The water was still in the bath, cold and unwelcoming, but she couldn't wait to run any more. The chill eased the ache in her, and she let the water lap over her as she lay with closed eyes.

She had not given in to him easily. Every instinct in her had warned her to keep her secrets, but in the end he had been too strong for her. It was years since she had been beaten like that; not since her father had taken his strap to her with monotonous regularity.

She could feel the tears trying to escape from under her closed lids, but she was damned if she would cry because of Blaise Westerbrook and what he had done to her.

She had been a fool to let him know that she had dreamt of marriage with him; she had always sworn to herself that she would never do that until she was certain how he felt. Why she had given him such a weapon to strike her with she had no idea, but in any event it was too late to worry about that now. He had gone for good.

She lay there until she started to shiver; then she got out of the bath slowly and put on her wrap, powdering her face so that Bessie should not notice the tear stains or the bruise on her cheek.

"He's here."

She turned abruptly as Bessie came into the bedroom, cautiously, as if she half-expected to find Westerbrook still there.

"He? Who?"

"Mr. Smith. He's due at two, you know."

"I won't see him now."

"I can't send him away."

"You'll have to. I've told you, I can't see him now."

"What'll he think? He won't come back again. There's others 'e can go to if you won't oblige."

"Then let him go elsewhere. I don't care."

"That won't pay the rent, me girl. What's the matter with you? Is it Lord What's-'is-name?"

"It's nothing. Get rid of Mr. Smith, or whoever he is."

"All right, if you say so. I 'opes you know what you're doing."

Bessie was back in five minutes, throwing up her hands.

"I've never 'eard such language before, and I've 'eard some language in me time, I can tell you. Foul-mouthed 'e was. You won't see 'im any more."

"It doesn't matter. There's plenty more like him."

"You quarrelled, did you? You and 'is lordship?"

"In a way."

"It'll blow over, these things do. To-morrow 'e'll be as lovey-dovey as ever. Send you roses, like as not, or maybe a new bracelet, eh?"

"He won't send me anything, Bessie, ever again. It's finished."

"Now, love, things ain't that bad. It'll be all right to-morrow."

"It won't. It's over, I tell you; finished for good."

Bessie Poke saw the misery in Candace and shuffled from one foot to the other. She knew what Candace had felt for the handsome nobleman; knew something of the dreams which she had nurtured. Not that Candace had said much, but Bessie understood her very well.

"Well, love, as you say; there's plenty more where 'e came from. Never does to fret about a man, you know."

"No, you're right." Candace sat up straighter and held out her glass. "Damn the lot of them, eh Bessie? Get me another gin. I think I'll get drunk to-night."

TEN

In spite of Sidney's disappearance and the devastating social consequences of it, Arthur Grey decreed that Sara's eighteenth birthday party should take place as planned.

"How can we?" Rachel swished her fan back and forth very rapidly to cool her face which was burning from the heat of the fire. "Do you think people will have forgotten so soon? I could not face it, Arthur. It must be called off. Arthur, are you listening?"

"Yes, my dear, of course."

"Then you will cancel the party?"

"No, Rachel, I will not." He said it very firmly, brooking no more arguments. "I am not going to spend the rest of my life avoiding people. What is done is done. The party will take place as planned."

And so on the following Saturday, No: 11, Candle Square prepared to receive its guests.

Sara's birthday was on Sunday, but Sundays were reserved for church and the reading of suitable books. Arthur was not really a stickler for the observance of the Sabbath, but a party on the Lord's Day was out of the question.

At eight precisely, Sara Lessingham came down the stairs to greet her guests. It was the hardest thing she had ever had to do, but she was determined to face the ordeal with such courage as she could muster. She was surprised to find that most of those invited actually came, and after the first dozen or so enquiring glances she found herself almost reconciled to the evening. The buffet was a great success and Rachel was preening herself at the compliments which came her way:

the free-flowing punch and wine was loosening both tongues and stiff conventions as dancing and games took the place of conversation.

When Arthur Grey suggested that the younger members of the party should play hide and seek, Sara tried to avoid it, but Grey would have none of that.

"Nonsense, m'dear, of course you must play. It's your party, you know. Be off with you. Basil is almost ready to start looking for you all."

After she had been discovered in the linen closet by Basil Rossman it was her turn to be the hunter, and then a lanky boy called Joseph Burnham bade his prey scatter whilst he counted up to a hundred.

Sara did not know what made her turn to the basement. She happened to be near the door leading down to the kitchens and stores, and on an impulse opened it and began the descent. She could hear cook and Laura talking in the kitchen, but Mrs. Tamworth might be called upon to get fresh supplies from the pantry, and so she turned in the opposite direction.

There was a long narrow passage leading off to the right. Sara recalled it vaguely from childhood, but she had not been down there for years. A small oil-lamp was hanging on the wall which she took down, walking gingerly along the stone-flagged corridor until she reached a door. She remembered that there was an old store-room down there; one which was never used nowadays. She expected it to be locked, but there was a fault on the catch and the door gave way to the pressure of her hand.

It was deadly cold inside, and at once she began to regret her chosen hiding-place. She held the lamp up, looking round at the damp walls and floor and the old sacks and boxes piled one on top of the other. At the far side there was a large trunk, dirty and rusted. She was about to turn away when she caught sight of a piece of coloured material peeping out from the lid. She hesitated, knowing she ought to go upstairs again away from the mouldering darkness of the cellar, but transfixed by the certain knowledge that the strip of cerise satin which she could see was not old like everything else in the store. It looked new and fresh, as if it had not been there very long, and slowly and reluctantly Sara moved towards the trunk and bent down to look at it.

She had been right. Her fingers touched the material hesitantly; it was new, or nearly so. She waited a long while before she opened the trunk, and then slowly she raised the lid. She stared down for one whole second at the contents, the light from the lamp not permitting her to miss one detail of the horror. Aggie Lowther's plump young body had been forced in at an uncomfortable angle, her head twisted on one side as her vacant eyes looked blankly upwards. The smell was appalling, and Sara's nerveless fingers dropped the lid with a sudden clatter, but not before she had seen her own scarf wound tightly round Aggie's neck. In that moment her mind was very clear. She could recall very precisely the day she had lost that scarf, for it had been a favourite one, and she had always been puzzled that neither she nor Jenny had been able to find it. Now she knew what had become of it, and her throat was so parched that she could not swallow.

Somehow she got out of the room and pulled the door closed behind her. Without realising it, she passed the kitchen door and went up the stairs and into the hall again. The sudden noise of music and voices was shattering, and she put the oil lamp down on a ledge and for a second covered her ears to stop the jangling din. She had no idea what to do. She knew she ought to tell Uncle Arthur immediately, but for some reason she could not bring herself to do it. It was her scarf round Aggie's neck, and everyone knew that she was peculiar. She had done some very strange things in the last few months; there was no doubt what people would say when they knew about Aggie.

She was standing still, her face blank with shock and desperation, when one of the hired maids came up to her.

"Miss Sara."

"Yes?"

"There's someone upstairs who wants to see you."

"Oh? Who . . . who is it?"

"Dunno, miss. I was just asked to say."

She nodded and was gone, for she had too much to do to stand about repeating her message, and Sara began to make her way towards the stairs. She thought someone spoke to her as she went, but she wasn't sure, and she didn't answer them. There was no one on the first floor; hide and seek was over, and the dancing had begun again. Then she began to look into the bedrooms, searching for whoever it was who had wished to speak to her. She thought perhaps Aunt Rachel had come up to rest and wanted to have a word with her, but Rachel wasn't in her room. She tried the others, but they were all empty, and so she went up to the second floor. This was deserted too, not a soul to be seen, not a room occupied.

She was standing outside the door of her own bedroom when she heard it. It came from the open archway, soft yet insistent, not to be ignored.

"Sara."

She could feel her whole body quivering and the candle which she had taken from her room was wavering in the draught. It must have been her imagination. There wouldn't be anyone up there; not to-night.

"Sara."

This time there was no mistake; someone was calling her name. She tried to move, but her feet were leaden.

"Sara, come up here."

She couldn't tell whether it was a man or a woman who was calling her. The voice was really not much more than a whisper, yet it had a penetrating quality for all that. She couldn't ignore it any longer, and although everything in her shrieked out to her to run, she went through the archway like a sleep-walker, mounting the stairs, feeling them give under the pressure of her foot.

"That's right, Sara, follow me. You know the room, don't

you? You've been in it before, haven't you?"

She went quietly and unresistingly into the attic room where she had seen the bed, and as she did so her candle went out in a sudden gust of wind.

"Never mind." The voice was consoling, still soft and muffled. "You won't need it again."

Sara stood very still in the darkness. She sensed the other person had gone over to the far side of the room, near to the bed, but in the pitch blackness she couldn't be sure. She was trying to pluck up enough courage to speak when the whisper began again.

"You've seen her, haven't you? I saw you go downstairs but I didn't think you'd try to hide in the old store. I knew she'd be found sooner or later if I couldn't move her, but there was no opportunity, you see. That's why she's still there, but if you hadn't gone down when you did, it might have been all right. I'd have got her away in the end, and I was sure that I'd locked the door."

"Who . . . who . . . are you?" Sara was trembling and her words quavered like an old woman's. "Who are you? What do you want?"

"It's your scarf, you know, did you notice? They'll say you did it, won't they? Everyone thinks you're a little mad already and now they'll know you are."

The whisper was oddly sexless. Sara strained her ears, trying to recognise something, anything, about it, but it was impossible. It was as if the person's head was covered with something which blanketed the personality behind it.

"But . . . I . . . I . . . didn't do it. How could I have done it?" Sara's breath was coming very rapidly, making her gasp as she protested her innocence. "I couldn't have carried Aggie to the cellar."

"You could have killed her downstairs."

"But I didn't . . . you know I didn't! Who are you?"

"They won't believe you. Better to die now than stand trial for murder. I've a draught here and some wine. You won't feel anything, I promise, and it'll be easier for you in the end. Do you know what they'd do to you after the trial?"

"No!" Sara's voice was louder, panic-stricken as she tried to back away. "I didn't kill Aggie. I wouldn't kill anyone. Who are you? Why do you hate me so?"

"Because you have everything."

"Everything? I have nothing . . . nothing at all."

"End it now." The whisper was more determined. "Everyone will understand. Poor Sara, they'll say; jilted at the altar and not quite right in the head. They'll understand."

"Who are you?" She almost screamed at the invisible tormentor on the other side of the room. "Mercy, is it you? Is it because I wouldn't marry Matthew? I couldn't marry him; I didn't love him."

"No pain at all."

"Henrietta, is it you? Do you hate me because you thought I would hurt Sidney? I know you didn't want me to marry him, but. . . ."

"Very quick, you won't feel anything."

Then the dreadful thought struck Sara and she put her hand to her mouth to stop the cry which welled up inside her.

"Sidney! It's you, isn't it? Yes, of course, it has to be." She knew the truth now, for Henrietta's warning was reverberating through her head. "Why did you run away? Why didn't you say you couldn't marry me; I would have understood. It was Uncle Arthur's idea, not mine. Have you been hiding here ever since the wedding day? Yes . . . yes . . . I suppose you must have been. But why did you kill Aggie? What had she done to you, Sidney?"

There was a faint laugh and then the door behind Sara blew shut with a loud slam.

She gasped and tried to run, but her feet wouldn't obey her. She could feel Sidney moving now, walking softly over the bare boards which sagged under his weight.

"No! No, don't come near me . . . don't come near me!"

She knew Sidney was closer now, for she could hear deep

breathing, and at last she managed to move, flinging herself against the door, hammering on it with her clenched fists.

When she felt the breath on the back of her neck she moaned and twisted away, stumbling in the inky darkness as she encountered a chair, almost falling over something rolled up in a bundle on the floor.

The whisperer turned too, following her as she struggled across the room whimpering and crying to herself, her throat closed as fear constricted it.

"Come here, Sara."

She gave a quick scream. Sidney was closer to her than she had realised, for the voice was not more than an inch or two away from her ear. She knew she had to push Sidney away, but when her fingers groped for his face it was not flesh she could feel but something soft and almost furry. Her terror was too deep to permit another cry, and she fell back on the bed as a hand fastened itself about her throat.

But then there was another noise as the door was thrown open again, crashing against the wall like thunder, and after that there were other sounds. Voices, normal voices, which gave brisk instructions, and footsteps and scufflings.

When the room came into view again in the light of the oil-lamps, Sara managed to pull herself up, holding her throat which ached with the pressure of deadly fingers. She was conscious of many things all at the same time. Incredibly, Blaise Westerbrook was there, and a man with a hard bowler hat, followed closely by two uniformed men. Blaise's face was white and angry, and he was staring at something as if he wanted to destroy it with his bare hands.

Then she turned her head, looking first at a pair of man's evening shoes, her eyes moving slowly upwards, past well-tailored trousers and a jacket with silk lapels, to the head which was covered with a dark cloth with slits where eyes glinted eerily. She moaned to herself, but then Blaise stepped forward and the cloth was pulled roughly off as she thrust her hand into her mouth to stop the agony which was pouring out of her.

The stolid-looking man in the bowler pushed gently past Westerbrook and said briskly:

"Arthur Grey, you're under arrest."

"But why? Why?"

Several hours later Sara was sitting in a deep armchair in the drawing-room of Blaise's house in Eaton Square. She was still cold in spite of the size of the fire and the large brandy which Blaise had made her drink.

"I don't understand. Why did he do it? Why did he hate me so?"

Westerbrook was lying back in his chair gazing at the flames.

"I don't think he did hate you. I think he was very fond of you."

"But how could he have been? He tried to kill me. Why?"

Blaise gave her a slight smile.

"That is what I asked myself when you first came to see me. Why? Not, of course, that I suspected then that Grey was involved or that he would try to kill you, but it was clear to me that if you were not mad, someone was up to something which was harmful to you. Augustine said there had to be a motive, and he was right, of course."

"Augustine?"

"My valet. I always talk to him; he is a very wise man."

"But how could there have been a motive? What reason was there for Uncle Arthur to do this?"

"Money. It is what Augustine and I first thought of, for it is the most obvious thing. Then we dismissed it, because we thought you had none."

"But I haven't. I've nothing except the small sum my father left for my upkeep."

"There is your legacy."

He saw her hazel eyes darken and wanted to lean forward to take her hand, but the moment was not right.

"But . . . but that is nothing." She shook her head. "You

must be wrong. Grandfather only left me a small remembrance. A trinket of some kind."

There was a brief silence between them, broken only by the crackling of the logs. Then Blaise said slowly:

"Rather more than that. Jason Lorrimer didn't lose everything as people supposed. He had seen trouble coming and had hidden away what he wanted you to have. He left you a fortune in diamonds, and Arthur Grey has been aware of that for years. He didn't know at first, of course. When he took you in, it was out of genuine compassion, and, although this sounds absurd, he was a good man in many ways. But then, a month or two before his death your grandfather wrote to you. You told me that only part of the letter was there, but Grey had seen it all. He has made a full confession. He kept that sheet to remind him of the name Westerbrook; someone to watch out for. It must have given him a bad moment when I first called to see him, but by then he'd had to learn self-control, and he didn't give himself away. Thank God he did keep part of the letter, for otherwise you would not have come to me."

Sara sank back, stunned to silence and Blaise gave a faint laugh.

"Yes, you're a rich girl, Sara Lessingham, and Grey knew it. With what he has told us, and from what we have learned from others, we have pieced the story together. Shall I tell you now, or would you rather wait until the morning?"

"No, no." She shuddered. "Tell me now please, I couldn't sleep yet. I should only think about...."

"Very well. Drink your brandy; it'll do you good." He took a sip from his own glass and looked back at the fire. "I think at first Grey was not unduly interested in the diamonds. He was prosperous; his business was doing well. He anticipated that by the time you were eighteen, he would be as rich as you, if not richer. But something went wrong with his business about a year ago; what, we are not sure. Furthermore, he was spending money like water."

"Uncle Arthur? But how? On running the house in Candle Square?"

Blaise shook his head wryly. "No, my dear, not on his house, although he was careful never to let Rachel or anyone else know that he was near to bankruptcy. He lived on credit to a large extent. No, he spent money on women and gambling."

"Women!" Sara gasped. "You must be mistaken. Uncle Arthur?"

"I'm not mistaken, I can assure you. Grey was always a womaniser. I only discovered that very recently, but as soon as I learned that he was not the man he purported to be, I began to see the first possibility of a solution. You see, I could not accept that you were unstable, Sara. I was sure that there was some other reason for the things which were happening, but I could get no hint of what or why until the other night. Once I knew the truth about Grey's women, and realised also that he was expecting to get a large sum of money from some source, I asked a lot of people questions, but it was only this afternoon that I found out the name of your grandfather's solicitor. Fortunately, his father knew mine, and I was able to persuade him to confirm what, by then, I half-suspected. I came as soon as I could and brought the police with me to confront Grey. I had not expected to find a party in progress; it was an inappropriate time for Grey to give one. Then I found neither you nor he were anywhere to be seen, and I feared I was too late. Thank God one of the maids told me someone had wanted to see you upstairs. It was a terrible moment for me, for I knew Grey had very little time left. If we had not reached you when we did, there would have been another accident or a suicide.

"I have just been able to get Mercy and Henrietta to tell me a few things too; they didn't want to, but I made them see how necessary it was and after all it was over for Grey by then. He always had to have women. He even seduced his own maids, up there in the attic, and Henrietta and Mercy knew it.

Sara stared at him.

"In the attic? Then there was a woman's wrap there and sheets and...."

"Oh yes, and that is why the stairs creaked at night. Nothing supernatural; just Grey and his lights-of-love. He'd been doing it for years. That's why he fostered the rumour that the house was haunted."

"I saw something once, when I was very young. It was the first Christmas I was here. I heard a noise and opened the bedroom door. There was a white figure holding a candle, moving through the archway. I've never forgotten it."

"Arthur's current mistress; one of the maids."

"But why didn't Mercy say something to someone if she knew? She made it seem as though the things which happened were my imagination."

"Because she is penniless. She relied on Grey for the very food she ate. Although nothing was ever said between them, Grey knew that she was aware of what was going on, and she knew that he expected her to protect him. It was Mercy who moved the wrap and sheets that day. She saw you rush down from the attic and went up to see what had frightened you. She locked the stuff in the room next door, so that when she offered to go up with you later, she knew there was nothing to see. She had grown to hate Grey, but there was nothing she could do about it."

"And Henrietta? If she realised what was going on, why didn't she tell Aunt Rachel?"

"She is fond of her father, although his weakness with women always upset her, but the real reason for her silence was that she feared that once Grey was exposed, the whole life of the family would collapse. She thought her father might even go away, leaving her and her mother to fend for themselves and she couldn't face the thought of that. She needed the warmth and protection of her good home and so she kept quiet."

"Poor Henrietta." Sara looked down at her hands. "No wonder she was so withdrawn and silent. But there were other things; things which I don't understand."

"Well, they're all capable of explanation." He smiled at her again, and in a way which made her head swim. "When Arthur began to realise that he needed your money, he decided that the easiest course was to get you married to Oliver or Sidney. Both of them were under his thumb and once you had married one of them, the money would have been as good as his, and he really didn't want to hurt you."

"But Oliver died."

"Yes, and Grey killed him."

"What!"

He looked at her shocked face and nodded.

"Yes, but it was an accident, of course. He was trying to kill Matthew Compton because he could see that Compton was becoming very interested in you, and he wasn't sure how you would respond. He says he followed Compton out of the house that night but lost him momentarily in the fog. Then he thought he saw him again and pushed him down the area steps, only it was Oliver he saw, not Compton."

"But . . . but . . . I can't believe it. Uncle Arthur was distracted with grief."

"Of course he was, he'd just killed his favourite son, but by then he knew he had to go on. He brought Sidney forward, but Matthew was still a nuisance. All this time Grey was trying to convince you, and others, that you were not quite normal. That was important, because you had to be persuaded that a safe marriage was your only hope outside an asylum. It was he who paid someone to push you off the pavement in Regent Street; he's told us that. He didn't intend to kill you, just to frighten you. He took you to see a woman in a mental hospital, didn't he? That was a warning too. He got rid of the maid, Jenny, whom we've traced, by the way. He thought she was too friendly with you, and might have helped you, so he planted his wife's ring in the girl's drawer."

"The razor? I didn't really try to kill myself, did I?"

"No. Grey contrived to slip a sleeping draught into your

drink that night. Then he crept in and made the mark on your wrist and left the razor near to your hand."

"Thank God."

"You should never have doubted yourself. I didn't, at least not for long."

She blushed and said hurriedly:

"What about Aggie? Did Uncle Arthur murder her too?"

"Yes, he was sleeping with her; it was her wrap which you found. He says she was getting above herself, demanding too much, and he thought she might have had an inkling about some of the things which were going on. When he dropped something into Compton's cup that day when he was taken ill, he says Aggie was looking at him very knowingly. After that she began to ask for clothes and money. He admits he took your scarf some time ago; he thought it might be useful to point to you, although it was later he knew he had to get rid of Aggie."

"Uncle Arthur tried to poison Matthew?"

"Well, he made him ill to scare him off. He hoped everyone would think you had had something to do with it, because by then his plans were working well. People were beginning to ask themselves questions about you."

"But how could he have done it in front of everyone? Where did he get the stuff to put into the cup?"

"You forget, Grey's business is chemicals and drugs, and as to how he did it, that was easier still. He was helping to pass the cups. Henrietta remembered that."

"Yet in the end Matthew died."

"Yes, he had to. Grey employed someone to find out more about Compton. When the man discovered that Compton worked in the solicitor's office where your grandfather's Will was lodged, Grey realised that Compton knew about the diamonds. Also, he suspected that Matthew had attacked Sidney to get him out of the way. Matthew wanted to marry you, you know."

"Simply because of the diamonds."

It wasn't a question, and Westerbrook laughed gently.

"There may have been other reasons. At any rate, Compton had to be disposed of, and again Grey paid a man to do it."

She gave a shuddering sigh.

"I simply cannot believe that Uncle Arthur would do such dreadful things. He was always so loving and so considerate."

"That was his real nature, and if he had not been faced with desperate money problems, and something else, he would probably never have harmed a fly as long as he lived. As it was, he was forced into becoming a monster, but it was a role he hated."

"You said money and something else? What else?"

She saw Blaise's face grow cold, almost frightened by the line of his mouth and the chill in his eyes.

"There was a woman." His voice was very quiet. "Not like Aggie and her predecessors. This woman is beautiful and Grey was in love with her. Indeed, it was more than mere love; it was an obsession. He was like a man with a fever which was burning him up. She is a prostitute, and very expensive. I should know." He gave Sara a straight look. "She was my mistress too, Sara, although I was never in love with her."

"I see."

She looked away quickly so that he should not see the hurt in her.

"I doubt if you do, but no matter. That old woman you saw."

"Yes?" Sara raised her head again. "That could not have been Uncle Arthur. She really existed then?"

"Oh yes, as large as life. This woman of whom I speak paid one of my maids to keep her informed about my affairs."

"So that she could blackmail you, you mean?"

"No, it wasn't that. It is poetic justice, in a way. Grey adored this woman, but she was in love with me. She wanted to know of everything that I did. When she heard a girl had called on me, and later found out that I had visited Candle Square, she was determined to find out who you were. Then she decided to do a little frightening of her own. She used to be an actress before she found an easier way to live. It was when she asked me to get something from a cupboard in her bedroom, and I found hidden there an old-fashioned bonnet sewn to a grey wig, that I first began to see some hope of getting to the bottom of all this. I forced her to tell me about it. She admits she was wildly jealous of you. She also wrote letters to you, I understand. You didn't tell me about those, Sara."

"No . . . no . . . I couldn't. They were too . . . too awful. I didn't understand all that they said, but I knew they were horrible. I couldn't bear to speak of them to anyone."

"I see." He hesitated as if he were considering whether to ask her more about the letters, but then he went on. "The woman found out quite by chance who Grey was; when she disguised herself and went to Candle Square. She was doubly-tied to you, through Grey and through me. It was she whom you saw at Christmas, outside the house. She wore a mask."

Sara's face was pinched. "I see. I was so frightened . . . I. . . ."

"Yes, I know." He said it curtly, not looking at her. "That is why when I questioned this woman I. . . ."

"What?"

"It is nothing."

"What about the matches in my drawer and the broken watch? This woman could not have been responsible for those."

"No, that was your cousin Rebecca. Henrietta guessed that, but she wouldn't speak about it. She was as frightened as you, in her way. She could see something very evil going on around her, but she is not used to confiding in people. She is a very self-contained person and she was terrified that if she once started to probe, the whole of her small world would crumble about her ears."

"I knew Rebecca was jealous of me. I think she wanted Matthew."

"I'm sure she did, but she's well-served by his death. He was almost as calculating as Arthur and his mistress, but not so clever."

"I cannot understand why uncle left Aggie's body in the house." Sara looked rather sick as she thought about the dead girl's bloated face and glaring eyes. "That was a terrible risk."

"Yes, and he knew it, but he had had no time to get it out of the house. He planned to move it next week, when I gather your aunt and cousins were to have gone to the country to visit friends."

"Yes, we were all going, but didn't he guess that someone would find it before then?"

"He had to gamble that they wouldn't and don't forget he was a gambling man. He had no idea the lock was broken, and no one goes to that store now, or so he told us."

"I did."

"Yes, and he happened to see your face when you got back to the hall. He realised then that you'd found Aggie, but in any event he had to do something about you to-night."

"It was . . . was . . . awful." Sara's fingers were gripped hard together. "I don't know why I went upstairs. I don't think I knew what I was doing. When I heard the whisper from the archway, I nearly fainted, but even then I could not stop myself."

"Don't think about it; it's over. Think about your missing bridegroom instead."

"Sidney!" Sara's mouth opened in consternation. "Oh, poor Sidney. I thought it was he upstairs, but afterwards I forgot all about him again."

"I am vastly reassured," said Blaise dryly, ignoring the question in her eyes. "Yes, I wondered when you would ask about him."

"But Uncle couldn't have killed him too. I suppose Sidney could not face marrying someone like me and so he ran away."

"No, he didn't. Sidney is not a coward, and he was only too willing to marry you. Sidney was abducted."

"Abducted!" She gaped at him, seeing his laughter and not understanding it. "What do you mean, abducted? How can he have been? Who would take Sidney?"

"I did." Then Blaise did lean forward to put his thin, strong hand over hers. "I had no intention of letting him marry you, Sara, and so I removed him. I intercepted his carriage and took him off. He's quite safe, although I'm afraid he's rather angry about the whole affair. He doesn't know about his father yet, of course. I shall have to tell him."

She tried to ignore the feel of his fingers on hers and returned to her questions.

"Why did Uncle Arthur try to kill me to-night. How would that have helped him, or was it just because I found Aggie?"

"No, your death was essential, since by your grandfather's Will, if you died without issue before your eighteenth birthday, your aunt would have received the diamonds. Your grandfather obviously did not approve of Grey, but when it came to it, he could not bring himself to leave his fortune to a stranger. He thought, of course, that as you were young and healthy when he last saw you, there would be no problem."

"I see, so that when Sidney disappeared, there was nothing else uncle could do. As soon as I became eighteen, I would have been told about grandfather's gift and uncle was afraid that I wouldn't marry Sidney, even if he were found."

"Precisely, although Grey says he had to assume that Sidney might be dead. He had to do something before to-morrow, or rather to-day. It was his last chance. He says he's been putting off the final moment as long as possible. In spite of everything, he has a great fondness for you."

"Poor Uncle Arthur. If only I had known, I would willingly have given him any money he wanted."

"He didn't know that, and besides he could never have brought himself to admit what kind of debts he had incurred, nor the company he was keeping. Grey kept the two halves of his life very much apart, as if he were two separate persons."

"Yes, he did. I had no idea that he cared about women at

all. Is she very beautiful?"

Westerbrook's mouth moved fractionally.

"Yes, she is."

"She must have loved you very much, otherwise she could not have done what she did."

"No, perhaps not."

Sara straightened her shoulders.

"Well, that is that. There is only one thing you cannot explain, Lord Westerbrook and that is probably because it is inexplicable."

"What is that?"

"Why I dream such terrible things. Perhaps it is because I killed my parents, although I don't remember anything about it."

"I have part of an answer for you; I told you I'd been asking questions. We found Mrs. Marsham, with whom you stayed after the fire. She says there was never any question of you having a box of matches. They knew how the fire started; it had nothing to do with you. No one knows what happened to you when the blaze began; they were afraid you had been trapped in one of the upper rooms. Then, when the fire was out, they discovered you kneeling beside the body of your mother. Her face had been burnt completely away, and you were holding what was left of her hand, crying and asking her to wake up. You must have run out of the house and returned later and found her, before the others could get to you. You were only seven at the time; no wonder that you dream."

She closed her eyes, burying her face in her hands.

"Sara." Westerbrook got up and came to her side. "My dear, don't . . . don't . . . it's all over now; the whole ugly mess. You must forget all about those things which Grey tried to make you believe about yourself. You didn't kill your parents, you didn't walk in your sleep, you don't see things which aren't there, and you are very lovely."

She looked up quickly, seeing the expression on his face and feeling her cheeks colour with nervousness.

"You are even more delightful when you blush." He pulled her gently to her feet. "I have admitted some of my sins to you; there are many more. Will it make a difference?"

"I . . . I don't think so."

"I hope not, because to-morrow there are other things I want to say to you."

"It is to-morrow now."

She said it shyly, hoping he would not think her too bold.

"So it is." He gave a soft laugh. "Then happy birthday, Sara Lessingham. Will you marry me?"

Candace Martin fastened the pearls about her neck and gazed at them admiringly in the mirror. In a moment she would ask John to bring the carriage round and then she would be off to Kate Hamilton's for an intimate little supper with Reginald Catesby. Reginald was portly, balding and rather dull, but he was excessively rich and very doting.

She touched her lips again with some more salve, running her tongue over them to make them shine. Yes, she really looked rather well to-night, and Reginald would be proud to be seen with a woman who attracted every man's eye.

She glanced at the opened letter by the powder bowl and her green eyes flickered momentarily. She had not expected to hear from Blaise Westerbrook again, least of all to receive an apology from him. She picked up the letter and tore it slowly and deliberately into shreds. She could live very well without Blaise Westerbrook and his apology, and she was grateful to him in a way, for he had taught her a lesson which all Marie-Amélia's lectures could not have done. She would never let herself love another man as long as she lived. She would go to Mayfair to-morrow to see Marie-Amélia. Perhaps she could live in Paris for a while; Blaise's generous cheque enclosed with his letter would set her up very nicely in some small hôtel in the fashionable quarter, and there would soon be plenty of men willing to pay the bills for her.

She picked up her cloak and went to the door, turning back

to look at the crimson curtains and the red and gold bedspread. Perhaps Blaise was right; maybe they were rather common. To-morrow she'd think about changing them again. Perhaps lilac and cream or turquoise and lemon; even silver and blue would be nice.

She would ask Reginald's opinion over supper. After all, he was going to pay for them.